Dark
Ride

For Anne McKay Green
1927–1989

Caroline Green is an experienced freelance journalist who has written stories since she was a little girl. She is a self-confessed 'book geek' and her first writing won the teen category of a competition run by Little Tiger Press at the Winchester Writers' Conference in 2009.

Caroline lives in North London with her husband, two sporty sons and one very bouncy labrador retriever.

Dark Ride

CAROLINE GREEN

PICCADILLY PRESS • LONDON

First published in Great Britain in 2011
by Piccadilly Press Ltd,
5 Castle Road, London NW1 8PR
www.piccadillypress.co.uk

Text copyright © Caroline Green, 2011

A catalogue record for this book is available
from the British Library

ISBN: 978 1 84812 138 6 (paperback)

1 3 5 7 9 10 8 6 4 2

Printed in the UK by CPI Bookmarque Ltd,
Croydon, CR1 4PD
Cover design by Simon Davis
Cover photo © Getty

CHAPTER 1

The Ticket

Welcome to Slumpton.

That's what the sign's meant to say but some of the letters have worn off. So all you really see is *Welcome to Slum*.

Hilarious, right? Or it would be, if you didn't have to live here.

I ran past the sign, not stopping until I could make out the slice of grey sea in the distance. The sound of Mum squawking like a constipated parrot was still ringing in my ears. 'I'm warning you, Bel!' and, 'Come back this minute, Bel!' and, 'I know I'm overreacting, Bel, but I'm your mother. It's my job!'

Okay, she didn't say the last bit. She never admits she's wrong. It was because I mentioned what a huge mistake

1

it was moving here that a row over nothing (Marmite contamination of the butter) turned into A Big Scene.

We had, 'You have no idea how hard it is for me!' and, 'The world doesn't revolve around you!' and then, 'It's not like your dad is here to help!'

That's when it got nasty. I probably shouldn't have said it was her fault for kicking him out. Her eyes went all bulgy, so I opened the front door and just ran. I didn't have a plan (or even a coat) but eventually I found myself at the top of the hill, the salty air scouring the inside of my lungs.

It had all started with a letter, plopping through the letterbox just like it really was a letter and not a bomb thrown into the centre of my life. At first, it seemed like good news. Mum's eyes shone when she told me she'd inherited a house by the seaside and all our money problems would be over. We even did a little dance. But all that was before she realised she wasn't allowed to sell it for a thousand years or something.

Or mentioned that Dad wasn't coming with us.

I told her in no uncertain terms that she was ruining my life, but it made no difference. I sobbed the whole time we were packing up the house.

It seemed like five minutes later we were here, the Land That Time Forgot, watching the removal van disappear round the corner like a last hope.

A week on from moving-in day, we were at each other's throats and nothing about living here had got any better.

Everything was buzzing like angry bees in my head as

I walked down the hill towards the promenade.

I came here often, grotty though it was. An amusement arcade was the only thing always open and a skinny teenage girl with angry eyes sat hunched in a booth at the entrance. I would have gone in to warm up but I'd been in once before and it smelled of fags and boys' socks.

I pulled my cardigan round my shoulders, wishing I'd thought to grab my fleece as I stormed out of the house. I walked along for a bit, past the boarded-up fish and chip stalls and popcorn stands, and past the hotel that looks really posh until you get close and see the way the paint's all scabby, like a skin disease.

'Just wait till summer,' Mum kept saying. 'Then you'll see how good it is here.' But the sea looked so cold and evil you couldn't imagine anyone putting on cozzies and slicing through it on bodyboards.

Tears prickled my eyes and I swiped my sleeve across them, quickly checking that no one was watching. I walked down to an old shelter which was splashed all over in pigeon poo, apart from one small bit. I sat down carefully and looked out to sea, sighing with my whole body.

I heard a cough then and turned round, startled.

He was slumped in the corner with his hood up. I stared at the side of his head for a minute and then he turned towards me, slowly. Eyes the colour of dark chocolate in a gaunt, pale face. A year or two older than me, but a lot taller.

'All right?' I said, but he just stared like I'd said

something really strange. I tutted and moved a bit further down the bench.

He leapt to his feet then and started walking away, head down and hands deep in his pockets.

I scowled and rubbed my goosepimply arms. Trust me to sit down next to a certified lunatic. Maybe that's what living here did to people. It wouldn't be long before I was mumbling to myself and sitting too close to people on buses.

Staring out to sea, I started thinking about what a pathetic figure I must be to anyone watching. They'd probably think I was homeless (which I practically was, when I considered what sort of reception I'd get when I got back) or had lost both my parents in a terrible car crash. I let the tragic feeling settle around me like a warm blanket, but my stomach started rumbling and I remembered I hadn't even eaten my toast, despite all the trouble the Marmite had caused. I knew I'd have to go home and face the music some time, so I got up.

That's when I noticed something next to me on the seat.

I picked up a small, blue ticket – the kind that comes from an old-fashioned roll. *Admit One* was written on it in black letters. The weird boy must have left it behind.

Sometimes I freeze-frame that moment in my mind. I could easily have left the ticket there on the bench and thought no more of it. But I didn't. For some reason I can't explain, I picked it up and slipped it in the pocket of my jeans.

Then I started the Walk of Doom home.

CHAPTER 2

Sunshine

I had to knock twice when I got back. Mum finally opened the door, frowning at the sight of her disappointing daughter. She didn't speak, but her eyebrows said, 'Don't think for a moment we're done, Annabelle, because I still have quite a lot to say on the matter. However, it will have to wait until later because someone is here just now and I don't wish to air my dirty laundry in public.' (I know. It's quite a skill.)

I followed her down the gloomy hallway, which was painted the colour of snot, and went into the warm, fuggy kitchen.

'Hello, Nell. Where have you been gadding off to then?'

It suddenly all made sense.

'Um, it's Bel, Mrs Longmeadow. Just been out for a walk.'

'Ooh, you'll catch your death on a day like this.'

Mrs Longmeadow, next-door neighbour and one-woman medical dictionary, sat at the table like a fat pigeon. She was clutching another one of her newspaper cuttings in her chubby little hands, which were knobbly with all the rings she liked to wear.

Mum gave me a desperate look. I could just make an excuse and go up to my room (which was about five times smaller than the one I'd had in London, I might add), but I knew that if I helped her out a bit, it might just get me some much needed credit.

I pulled up a chair.

Mum didn't go as far as smiling or anything insane but I knew she was pleased.

'I was just asking your mother whether she knew much about cholesterol medication,' said Mrs Longmeadow. 'I've been reading about side effects and I'm sure that my doctor isn't all he should be. He's, you know . . .' She hesitated and then mouthed the word 'foreign'.

'Uh-huh,' I said, nodding vigorously. I might have overdone it a bit because Mrs L gave me a strange look, but she soon picked up where she left off. I tuned her out and noticed Mum escaping with a basket of washing under one arm.

Mum used to work on reception in a doctor's surgery, but for Mrs L this was as good as being a top brain surgeon. She usually came to the door clutching a cutting from the *Daily Mail* and asking Mum if she knew anything about this or that medical yuckiness.

She kept droning on and I started thinking about the strange boy from earlier. I wondered if he was homeless and I shivered, remembering how cold it had been out there. After a few minutes, I tuned back into Mrs L, who was still in full flow. I sometimes entertained myself when she was in one of her rants, just to spice things up. I couldn't resist making one eyeball wander a tiny bit.

'You want to get that checked out,' she said, narrowing her own watery blue eyes.

'What's that then, Mrs Longmeadow?' I said innocently.

Mrs L regarded me warily. She had a way of looking at you, like you were something dodgy she'd picked up on the bottom of her high-heeled shoe. (She had tiny, fat feet. Practically hooves.)

'I'd best be getting on,' she said finally, with a loud sniff. 'My son and grandson are moving in today and I have things to do.' She stuck her chest out. 'My son's a journalist,' she added. Like I cared.

'MUUUUM!' I yelled, making her jump. I smiled my sweetest smile. 'Mrs Longmeadow's leaving now.'

I couldn't sleep that night. I lay for hours thinking about London, my old bedroom and the Dad-shaped hole in my life. When I did finally drop off, I had horrible dreams about walking into the cold sea and hands pulling me under the water.

When I woke up my heart was doing a tango. For a

minute, I thought I was back in my old house and could almost hear Dad humming in the shower (he's always humming, strumming his guitar, or singing). But instead of looking at the bright blue ceiling of my old room, I was staring up at the old-lady wallpaper on the sloping roof above the bed. (Mum promised we'd decorate just as soon as we could afford it, but nothing would make this room nice. Except maybe a bulldozer.) There was no singing from the bathroom, just the plip-plopping of a leaky tap.

I heaved a big sigh and swung my legs into the Arctic tundra. It was always freezing here. We moved two weeks before the Christmas holidays, like no one else in the world does. Other people move at sensible times like summer or never. I got a little whump in my chest thinking of Jasmine and Molly, Christmas shopping at Wood Green without me. They'd both texted a few times, but I was too miserable to reply properly – I'd just sent short answers back, not really letting on how I was feeling. It had been a few days now and I'd heard nothing more from them. Maybe they were forgetting about me already.

By the time I'd been to the loo, brushed my teeth and got dressed, my imagination had them giggling over steaming hot chocolates in the shopping centre. 'Bel who?' they'd say if anyone asked.

It would be like I never existed.

I came into the kitchen. The décor was even worse in there. The walls were green with big swirly purple bits on it that made your eyes go funny.

Mum started to say, 'Good morning' and then clocked

my expression. She turned back to the sandwiches she was packing into her lunchbox. I grunted and sat down at the table, before shaking some cornflakes into a bowl. We always had the cheapest own-brand ones now. (Mum always said they all came from the same factory anyway. I always said, 'Well, how come these ones taste like toenails and cardboard?') She had some kind of office job at the Town Hall, but we still never seemed to have any money.

'The school holidays have started now,' said Mum, in a fake cheerful way. 'You might find a few more people your own age about the place.' She turned to look at me and sighed, then pointed at a piece of paper pinned with the banana magnet to the board. 'I've left a few chores for you.'

I grunted again and shovelled in the cereal. Mum left the room. She came back wearing her warm black coat and red scarf, which looked nice with her hair. It's what you'd call dark auburn, but what she passed onto me is more like ginger, whatever she says. And whereas hers falls in obedient curls around her face, mine has a life of its own. It's not her fault really. But it feels like it's her fault.

I noticed she had lots of lines around her eyes that never used to be there.

'I'll be back at five-thirty, okay?' she said and I nodded, distantly.

She patted the top of my head. 'Be good, Bel, and stay close to home.'

Home? This would never be my home.

CHAPTER 3

A Taste of the Med

I know Mum hates to leave me on my own when she goes to work, and never did it in London, but at fourteen I was too old for a childminder and the only other option was to sit next door with Mrs Longmeadow. If I said I'd rather poke needles into my eyes, you'd get the picture. Luckily, Mum didn't force me.

Often I'd just go back to bed and read, or watch daytime telly until she got back. There wasn't anything else to do. We were waiting to get our broadband sorted so I couldn't even go online. But as I looked round the poky kitchen that morning, a horrible feeling of panic pressed in all around me.

I had to get out.

I grabbed the list of shopping from the board and

shoved it into my pocket. This time I made sure I put on my warmest jacket and pulled my favourite blue hat down over my disobedient hair, before grabbing my keys.

I felt a bit better as soon as I was outside and slowed my steps as I walked down the road.

I like to look through windows of houses as I pass them. Most have net curtains up, but there was one at the end of the street where you could see right in and it looked really cosy. A fat orange cat slept on the table and there was a piano and a big squashy sofa with red tasselled cushions. It didn't actually have a roaring fire in a fireplace, but looked like it should, and I always imagined there would be yummy cake-baking smells inside.

I stopped to have my usual nosy and a girl's face appeared right in front of me. She just popped up like a jack-in-the-box. I sort of went, 'Wah!' and we stared at each other for a moment with circle mouths.

She was about my age, with long blond hair and trendy glasses with black rectangular frames. I blushed and scurried down the street, feeling really silly. She'd probably think I was some sort of stalker-nutter.

It was only when I got down to the seafront again that I realised I had no idea where I was going. I stood there for a minute, not sure what to do with myself. A dirty great seagull swooped down in front of me and looked at me with its beady little eyes. It opened its beak and screeched. It sounded like it was saying, 'Alone! *Crark!* Alone!'

I mumbled, 'Get lost' and kicked out, making it flap away.

I stared out to sea. The water was choppy today. Rough green waves rolled over and over and sucked at the tiny strip of beach. I say 'beach' but to me that's something with rippling golden sand, where you stretch out your towel or build sandcastles, but this one was covered in little sharp stones that stuck to your shoes and seemed to pull at your feet as though they wanted to drag you down and choke you.

Everything was grey – the sea, the sky, the buildings. You could see that some of the buildings on the seafront had been painted yellow once, but really they were just a different kind of grey now. The wind felt like bony fingers raking my cheeks. I bowed my head into it and started to go in the usual direction, but, glancing up, I thought I could see the blob-shape of Mrs Longmeadow ahead with her tartan shopping trolley. I spun round and hurried in the other direction, away from the town centre.

There weren't many people about. A man and a woman huddled in big puffa jackets passed and the woman glanced at me. She had panda circles under her eyes and it was impossible to tell if she was twenty or fifty. I wondered if she was a druggie. I wouldn't have been surprised. It was that kind of a place. I'd gone for a wee in the Morrison's toilets the week before while Mum was shopping. The light in there was this weird neon purple. For a minute I thought aliens were going to start experimenting on my brain or something. Mum told me later that it was a special light that stopped smackheads from being able to see their veins. Nice. I bet they don't put *that* on the tourist information.

I knew Dad would hate it here. He grew up in the country, unlike Mum. She had often talked about us 'getting away from it all' and moving out of London and he'd always say, 'Getting away isn't all it's cracked up to be, hon.'

I wondered where he was at that exact moment. Probably sleeping off the gig the night before with the other guys and wishing he could come home. I hadn't heard from him for over a week and the thought made me shiver, even though I knew he was on tour.

But I'd heard the shouting before he went. I knew she didn't want him around.

I gave myself a shake. Dad wouldn't want me to be moping all over the place. He'd probably start tickling me or say something silly. I had to stay strong for him, even though my life was ruined.

The houses were thinning out now. A bit further up on the seafront there was a huge building site, surrounded by hoardings.

I stood back to look at the giant poster stuck up there. *A Taste of the Med* was in massive letters across the top, and underneath there were pictures of couples clinking glasses in restaurants and a smiling girl running on the sand with a big red kite. Her good-looking mum and dad were holding hands behind her and laughing. A carrier bag had somehow got stuck up there, flapping about

13

madly like it was attached to the dad's head and there was a big glop of bird poo dripping down the girl's face.

Along the bottom of the billboard were the words, *Dolphin Marina. Open Soon.* Well, they were a bit behind on that one, because so far, all there was to show was a poster. I wished they'd hurry up with it. Maybe I could run along the beach with a red kite and my mum and dad would be holding hands and grinning their heads off behind me.

I swallowed hard and was just turning for home when I got a prickling sensation up my spine and over my scalp, like someone was watching me. I did a quick scan but nobody was around. I called out a shaky, 'Hello?' but my voice seemed to bounce back, mocking me. I turned a full circle one more time and that's when I saw someone sitting on the sea wall a bit further up. I couldn't understand why I missed them the first time.

The lean figure was strangely familiar and I realised it was the weird boy from the bus shelter the day before. Without turning round, he got up and started to walk along the wall, fast and easy, in that long-leggedy way some boys have. He leapt down and carried on walking, head down into the biting wind. Something was glinting on the ground near where he'd landed and I walked over to it, curious. It was catching the light and sending little sparkles towards me, even though the sun was swallowed up in grey winter cloud.

I bent down. It was a small bunch of keys. They were attached to a tiny wooden keyring in the shape of a

Russian doll, painted blue with lots of white and red spots. It seemed a girly sort of a keyring for a boy to have.

I looked up and shouted, 'Hey!' but he didn't hear me and carried on walking quickly away. I looked at the keys again. Better give them back. His front door key was probably on there. Not really knowing why I should care either way, I followed him.

I had to run a little bit because he was moving so fast, but he didn't turn round, just kept marching on with his head bowed into the wind. My cheeks were stinging and my knuckles were raw, but I kept on going. I didn't even know why I was following him. He was starting to annoy me now. I began to jog to catch up, past some horrible public toilets that were blasting their wee smell to the world.

I came to an old fairground with *Do Not Enter – Condemned Property* plastered all over it. The entrance was a big semicircle, painted like a sun shining, but worn away to a dirty yellow. *Sunshine Park* said the sign. There were two turnstiles with booths on either side, where people must have once sold tickets. The windows were broken and a delicate cobweb was stretched across one, as though holding the whole cabin together.

A shiver crawled up my spine. It felt like the most run-down, lonely place in the world. For a second, I thought I caught a musical snatch of voices in the air but it was just the wind whistling through cracks on the hoardings.

My instincts were practically holding up banners

saying, *RUN AWAY, BEL! RUN AWAY AND NEVER RETURN!*

But instead my fingers went into the pocket of my jeans and closed around the small piece of paper.

Admit One.

I looked at the faded blue ticket in my hand, the one I'd picked up the day before and slid it into the gap at the front of the turnstile as though by instinct.

Clunk.

The spiky bars of the gate whirled round, inviting me in, as I'd somehow known they would.

CHAPTER 4

Scooby Doo, Where Are You?

I regretted it precisely one second later.

I turned back, pushing the rusty metal turnstile, but it didn't budge. I thought about clambering over it but I'm rubbish at things like that and knew I'd probably get stuck halfway or something hideous. Okay, Bel, I thought, let's not freak here. Just think. It was probably like London Zoo. You came in one set of gates and had to go out through another.

I just had to find the exit.

And remember to breathe.

Moving slowly forwards, I looked around. There were boarded-up stalls everywhere and rubbish was blowing around on the muddy ground, which once must have been flattened by feet. Now there were lumps of grass breaking through, like nature wanted it back.

Up ahead was a long, low building with pictures of ghosts and bats painted on the outside. *GH ST TR IN* read a sign in red, the missing letters like gaps in teeth. The entrance was covered in long black sheets of plastic, which seemed to shiver a bit in the breeze.

It was just a cheesy old ghost train. So how come it was suddenly the scariest thing in the world? I scurried past, my teeth beginning to clack together in fright, wondering where Scooby and Shaggy were when you really needed them.

Looming over me were the metal tracks of an old rollercoaster, curving into the sky like the ribcage of a huge dinosaur. I could see a big wheel just beyond, with seats in faded yellows and greens that swayed gently and made ominous creaking sounds.

Over to the right, past a series of round stalls, I could see a splintery, faded sign in the shape of a finger marked, *Exit This Way*. I walked a bit quicker, desperate to run, but knowing that if I did, full-blown panic would kick in and I really would lose the plot.

Just at that moment, something happened that made every tiny hair on my body stand to attention.

I could hear music.

Plinky-plonky, old-fashioned music coming from just around the corner. Fear washed over me and I thought maybe I'd gone mad or was dreaming, but no such luck. This really was happening, right now. I sidled up to one of the round stalls, heart banging, and peeked around.

Light was blazing from an old-fashioned carousel, turning circles of gold and yellow, studded with red and blue light-bulbs. Tatty horses with mad, staring eyes gently swung around and up and down. My heart was beating so hard it hurt. I bit down on my trembling fingers. Some crazy axe murderer was about to leap out and finish me off, I knew it. Not a single soul in the world knew I was here, so they probably wouldn't find my mangled body for ages. My killer would probably be known as The Fairground Butcher. (I knew about these things. I'd seen *CSI*.)

Tears zigzagged my vision as I squinted hard into the harsh light.

Then I saw someone was on the carousel, looping around the horses like it was the easiest thing in the world. It was that boy again. I'd almost forgotten about him in the whole fearing-for-my-life business. He didn't look like an axe murderer. Just a tall, thin boy in a hoodie. I came out from behind the stall just as the carousel swung him in front of me.

His mouth dropped open and he let rip. 'What are you doing, sneaking up on me like that? How'd you even get in here?'

'I've as much right as you! Which is none!'

We exchanged glass-hard stares and then a smile started to curl around his mouth. He was one of those people who completely changes when they smile. Like the sun had come out.

'Stroppy, aren't you?' he said. 'How did you get in here, anyway?'

'I found a ticket,' I said. 'You left it. I saw you yesterday in that bus shelter. You left a ticket on the bench.'

His smile faded. 'I didn't leave any ticket,' he said after a moment.

'Okay, whatever, but that's how I got in,' I said.

He stared at me again. 'What's your name?'

'Bel,' I said.

'Bel? What kind of a name is *Bel*?'

'It's short for Annabelle, if you must know. But I'll have to kill you if you call me that.'

His mouth twitched and he nodded his head but didn't reply. Silence stretched between us like a giant piece of elastic.

'The other person says their name now . . .' I said, exasperated. 'That's how it works!'

'Luka,' he said, smiling again. 'It's Luka.'

'What kind of a name is Luka?' I smiled as I said it, but his face hardened.

'It's a Croatian name. My mum's from Croatia.'

Like I'd said something rude. What an annoying boy. I put my hand in my pocket.

'Look, you dropped these.' I held out the keys and his hand shot out to snatch them before I could blink.

'Have you been through my pockets or something?' he said and I was too insulted to answer.

I'd had enough of this nut-job. I was cold and hungry. And leaving. I started to walk towards the exit sign. Then all of a sudden he was right beside me, striding along in that loose-limbed way.

'Sorry,' he said. 'I expect I just dropped them.'

'Yes, I expect you did,' I said icily. 'Bit of a girly keyring that, isn't it?'

'It's my mum's,' he said, looking at me with the same expression as the day before. Like he was trying to see inside my head. It was very unnerving. 'It's a good luck charm, if you must know.' He ran his hand across his face, gave a half-hearted wave and said, 'Gotta go. Seeya.'

I shouted, 'Hey!' but within about ten seconds he had disappeared deeper into the fairground, leaving me standing there with leaves and rubbish all blowing around me.

I hadn't even noticed the music had stopped until now. It was deathly quiet. I felt like the only person in the world. Something moved at the corner of my eye and I spun round, but there was nothing there.

I hurried towards the exit. To my relief, the turnstile gate swung open as I pushed against it and I was soon outside, trying to catch my breath.

Mum wasn't back when I got home. I put the radio on, loud. I felt jumpy and strange. So far I'd met two people in this town, one horrible (Mrs Longmeadow) and one weird. It didn't bode well for the rest of my life here. I wondered again if Luka was homeless and had a sudden image of him bedding down in some doorway. On the other hand, maybe he was sitting down right now to a huge plate of bacon and eggs, his smiling mum and dad asking him all about his morning. I wondered what he'd say. ('Oh, I met this ugly girl, hung around a creepy old fairground and completely freaked her out, just for the hell of it.')

I sagged into a chair in the kitchen, suddenly missing Dad so much it made my teeth ache. We hadn't spoken for about a week.

Mum told me he'd had his mobile nicked and was getting a new one. That was why he hadn't rung, she said. We didn't have another number for him – Dad's band, Kasbah, was on tour somewhere up North and I knew they didn't stay in one place long.

But I couldn't stand not speaking to him for a moment longer. Even trying his old number was better than nothing, just for the feel of the familiar digits.

My fingers trembled as I dialled. Maybe the thief would pick up and I could give him a piece of my mind. It rang about four times and was about to go to voicemail. But just at that moment, someone picked up.

'Look, I'll call back when I get . . . Uh, hello?'

I almost dropped the phone. 'Dad?' I said. Happiness bloomed inside my chest.

'Bel, sweetheart . . .'

'You got your phone back! Dad, it's so good to hear your voice! Where are you now?'

'I'm just outside Leeds,' he said. 'Got my phone back this morning. Look, Bel, sweets, I'm in the middle of rehearsals. I'll call you tonight, okay?' And the line went dead. I put the phone down slowly.

I stood there for a moment, staring down at the telephone like it might still deliver something better.

Heaving a big sigh, I sat down on the bottom step of the stairs and tried not to feel hurt. Dad was just focused on the rehearsals.

He once told me that when you had a passion for something, like his music, you could lose yourself in it so completely that you'd forget about all the boring, mundane stuff in your life. It was a bit like flying, he said.

It made me feel funny when he said that, and envious too. Like I envied the music for having him, and envied him for having the music.

The phone rang late.

I could hear the low rumble of Mum's voice and crept out of bed to hover on the landing.

'You haven't spoken to her for a week and then you decide to ring when she's asleep. Honestly, Steve, do you ever think?'

There was a pause.

'Well, you've only got yourself to blame for that . . .'

I started to come down the stairs, and Mum turned round, frowning. 'Well, here she is, anyway. You might as well speak to her now you've got her out of bed.'

She handed me the phone. 'Don't stay on for long,' she said and clomped back upstairs.

I was set to be cool and distant with Dad, in revenge

for abandoning me and then being weird on the phone, but as soon as he spoke, I felt all my armour melt away.

'How's my Jelly-Belly then?' His voice was warm and fuzzy.

'Da-ad!' I said. I always pretended to mind that silly name, but hearing it felt like a hug.

'Sorry to call so late, sweetpea,' he said, 'but this is the first chance I've had. How you settling in on the Costa Del Kent?'

'I hate it,' I said with a big sigh. 'It'll be better when you get here though. When are you coming?'

He hesitated. I heard the pop of him sucking on his cigarette.

'Things are a bit complicated right now, Bel. With me and Mum. And what with the tour and all, I can't make any promises just yet.'

'But you're here for Christmas, right?' I hated the babyish whine in my voice but couldn't help it. The pause that followed made my heart sag into my stomach.

'Well, I needed to talk to you about that. We've been offered a gig in Scotland on Christmas Eve. Glasgow. It's good money and I can't really turn it down right now. But I'll try and get there on Christmas Day somehow. Or Boxing Day, okay? Bel?'

All I could do was make snuffly-snotty noises down the phone.

'Oh honey, please don't cry! I can't stand it. Please! Look, baby girl . . . I miss you every minute of every day. Once all this is over, I promise to make it up to you. We'll do something really good, just the two of us. It'll be like old times. In the meantime, you've just got to stay strong. Now dry your tears and hop back into bed. You don't want to look like Kermit the frog after a night on the tiles, do you?'

I gave a little hiccup and laugh all at once.

'That's a good girl. Got to stay strong for me. You get back into that bed now.'

A pause.

'G'night, baby.' *Click.*

CHAPTER 5

Christmas Lights

I swear I hadn't had a wink of sleep until just before Mum came into the room the next morning. My bottom lip was smushed against the pillow and I opened one eye. She gazed down at me and stroked a bit of my hair away.

'I'm on a half day today so I thought you could meet me from work,' she said. 'We can have lunch together and then do a bit of shopping, okay?'

'Gur.'

I was trying to say, 'Yes, mother, that sounds fine, although I am rather tired just now.' But 'Gur' was the best I could do.

She smiled. 'Meet me outside the Town Hall at twelve.' She started to bend down as though going in for a kiss, but something made her hesitate and she just patted my hair and left the room.

Maybe it was my morning breath.

On the other hand . . . maybe it was something to do with the last time she'd tried to be affectionate.

It was the day we were moving. Mum found me sniffling in my bedroom. I'd been having a last look round and found an old photo when they moved my bed out. It was a picture of Mum and Dad with me as a baby. Dad was looking at the camera and Mum was gazing at him like she was about to collapse laughing at any moment. He'd obviously just said something daft. They looked so happy. Anyway, when she came in, she saw the photo in my hand and tried to put her arms round me, but I'd shoved her away and said, 'Let's go, if we're going.'

I rolled over the memory and went back to sleep.

I was conked out until gone ten. My head was all woolly when I finally got up. I pulled on some warm things and brushed my teeth in the freezing bathroom, the tap drip-drop-dripping in the background.

The first thing I noticed outside was a big people carrier parked by Mrs Longmeadow's. Maybe she'd offered someone her life savings to come round and listen to her talk.

The second thing was that the sun was ACTUALLY OUT.

Slumpton looked much nicer under blue sky. I could

feel my spirits rising like a balloon as I walked towards what passed for a town centre.

The feeling didn't last long. The Christmas decorations in the shop windows were sparkling in the sunlight and all the trees had little fairy lights.

Don't get me wrong. Normally, I love Christmas. We'd always have a real tree and the three of us would decorate it together. Dad would sing along in a funny old-fashioned way to our CD of Christmassy songs and Mum would sometimes join in. It wasn't always perfect though. Last year they had a row about the way the decorations had been packed away, both blaming each other for the broken bits in the bottom of the box, which Mum cut her thumb on. It wasn't the best. But it was better than the thought of me and Mum facing each other over the turkey on our own.

I tried to force all thoughts of Christmas out of my head. Which wasn't easy when there was tinsel and cheesy snowmen in all the shop windows. I put my head down and ploughed through the shoppers (all ten of them) towards the Town Hall.

I passed through a small square where a small brass band was playing carols. I stopped to listen, despite myself. 'O Little Town of Bethlehem', rich and trumpety, filled the air and a memory so powerful popped into my head that for a minute I was right back inside my old life.

Last Christmas.

My class was practising for a carol concert. Ryan Smith's voice was breaking and kept going from a squeak to a growl and then back again. It was so funny that even Mrs Radley was in fits. Standing there in the main hall, with all the decorations up, laughing, I felt connected to everyone. Like we were lights on a Christmas tree.

It wasn't going too well, my not-thinking-about-Christmas policy. I sighed and turned to cross the road.

I looked up at the Town Hall – pale stone, sweeping steps and big columns all over the place. Sparkling in the sunshine, it looked like it should be somewhere grander, like London or New York. I leaned back against the wall and watched people coming in and out, my breath making hazy puffs in the cold air.

Mum appeared at the entrance after a few minutes, at the same time as a group of men. One of them was tall and broad, with close-cropped hair. He had an air of authority about him and a tan which surely hadn't come from Slumpton. His suit was lighter coloured than the others and he wore a brightly coloured tie. Next to him was a thickset man with no neck, who was speaking into his phone. Tanned Man held the door open for Mum and they exchanged a few words and laughed, then with a wave of his hand, he and his companions all swept down the stairs past me. Mum was knotting her scarf around her neck and her smile faltered when she saw me.

'Hi! Been waiting long?'

'Who was that?' I said and she blinked, then turned to look at where she'd just come out in a really obvious way.

'Who? Oh, that was Mr McAllistair, a local businessman who's involved in the marina project. He's very charming.' She said it like I should be impressed.

'Hmm,' I said meanly. 'Horrible suit.'

Mum's eyes narrowed. 'It's a very expensive suit, actually, Bel. I think he dresses very well.'

I thought of the clothes Dad wears: T-shirts with things like *The Ramones* or *The Smiths* on them, black jeans and red Converses. He has soft brown curls and soft brown eyes and Nan used to say, 'Handsome is as handsome does'. I didn't know what it meant but you could tell it wasn't good. She never said anything mean to his face, but she didn't approve of him being a musician and smoking and not working in an office like boring other dads.

And then Mum expected him to be completely heartbroken when Nan died! I mean, I'm sorry . . . I loved my granny and I cried loads when she had a heart attack and died so suddenly like that. But Dad had a really late night at a gig the night before the funeral and got up a bit late and hadn't picked up his one and only suit from the dry cleaners . . . and Mum started screaming at him about being useless and unfeeling!

Anyway, at least he knows how to look good. He wouldn't be seen dead in that horrible suit.

'Dad wouldn't be seen dead in that horrible suit,' I said.

Mum sighed. 'No, Bel. I don't suppose he would.'

We had lunch in a café inside Slumpton's only department store. Christmas was so in my face I could barely look at my baked potato with cheese and beans, jam doughnut and hot chocolate with extra whipped cream. But I managed to force them down. We were by a window, looking over the high street and something made me stand up quickly, almost knocking over my cup.

'Careful!' said Mum. 'What are you looking at?'

I was sure I had just seen Luka again – a lone, lean figure weaving through the crowd. I searched the shoppers below but he'd gone.

'Nothing,' I said, sitting back down again, and dabbing at the spilled chocolate with a napkin. 'Just thought I saw someone I know.'

Mum beamed. 'Oh, I'm so glad to hear you're making friends. Is she nice?'

'He,' I said, and her smile slipped. 'It's a he and I wouldn't exactly call him a friend. He's a complete weirdo I keep bumping into. I think he's stalking me, as a matter of fact.' I didn't really know why I said that. It wasn't like he'd done anything wrong really, apart from be a bit weird.

'Stalking you? I see. Is that why he's down there going about his business and you're almost hanging out of the window three storeys up?'

I tutted. 'It's not what you think, Mum,' I said but she just smiled.

She'd never understand. I'm not even sure I did. Luka wasn't like anyone I'd ever met before. My friends are always conscious of what people think of them. As though life is something that has an audience. It's just how we are with each other. (Or were, when I had friends.) But he didn't seem to care about that. It was like he was in a world of his own. Hanging around abandoned fairgrounds and ignoring people when he felt like it. I wondered where he went to school . . .

Uh-oh. Now I'd done it.

That was another thought that I'd been trying to push to the darkest corners of my mind.

January 4.

D-Day.

The day I started at David Stafford, my new school, with its nasty purple uniform that would never, ever look right. The thought made my stomach twist into an icy knot and pictures came rushing into my head.

Walking into the new classroom with people who'd known each other since they were four all staring at me.

Me standing alone at break time, while girls whispered and pointed in the playground.

Me crying myself to sleep at night, destined to be alone, shunned forever and . . .

'Bel? Are you listening to a word I'm saying?'

'Huh? What?'

Mum's eyebrows were almost crawling into her hair.

'I'm trying to talk to you! Really, Bel, I don't know why I bother sometimes.' This was followed by one of her Big Sighs. She sounded like a broken accordion lately.

I wanted to say I didn't know why she bothered either, but I kept quiet.

'Come on,' she said in a weary voice. 'Let's go.'

I put on my fleece and scarf again, still thinking about

school. Luka was bound to go to David Stafford. It was such a small town. Having one familiar face, even if he was probably a year ahead of me, was better than nothing. And I did help him find his key, even if he was supremely ungrateful and weird about it. Desperate times call for desperate measures and even though he would probably be rude again, so far Luka was the only person in Slumpton under a hundred years old I'd even had a conversation with.

I decided he probably deserved another chance.

CHAPTER 6

Gh st Tr in

I went looking for him the next morning. I knew that if I stayed still for too long, my brain would rattle with missing Dad and thinking about school. Better to be doing something, even if it was looking for weird possibly homeless boys.

Not that he was easy to find. First, I checked the shelter where I'd first seen him. All I saw was an old lady with a small brown dog she kept yanking like a conker on string.

There was nothing else for it. I'd just have to go back to that creepy old fairground. On the way I passed the marina development. I could hear lots of building noises coming from inside the high wooden fences. A sleek black car drew up and a man in a smart grey coat climbed out of the driver's side. He had a head like a bullet with no neck and close-cropped hair. I realised I'd seen him before, at the Town Hall. He paused and stared at me, rudely, as though I had no right to be there, then went round to the other side at the back and opened the door. Sure enough, the other man, Mr McAllistair, climbed out, speaking into his mobile. He gave me a sharp look too and I put my head down and scurried away. There was something a bit menacing about both of them.

It was only when I got to the turnstile that I realised the ticket had been swallowed up before and I couldn't get in. I gave one of the bars a little push, but it didn't budge. It was a stupid idea anyway. I didn't even know why I had come. I put my hands deep into my pockets and turned away.

But someone was suddenly right there next to me and I cried out, falling against the gates and my heart ba-booming like crazy.

'You nearly frightened me to death!'

'Got you back for the other day, then!' He stopped smiling when he saw I was rubbing my side. 'Sorry.'

'Yeah, right.'

Now he was here, I didn't have a clue what to say. I didn't want him to think I was looking for him.

'Looking for me?'

'Uh, no!' I said, my treacherous face burning straight away.

He just grinned, annoyingly. 'So how's it going, Aa-nnaaa-belle?'

'I told you not to call me that!'

He laughed. 'Sorry, you just look funny when you're angry. Like this . . .' He made a hideous face.

I couldn't help it; I burst out laughing. 'Shut up!' I said. Now that I was looking at him properly, I noticed his long dark eyelashes. It was suddenly really hard to look him in the eye and I blushed a bit, staring down at my feet.

'Fancy coming inside and having a look around?' he said, putting me out of my misery. But something held me back. I looked through the turnstile at all the boarded-up stalls inside. There was something about this place.

'I'm not sure . . .'

'Suit yourself,' he said crisply and neatly vaulted the turnstile.

'Wait!' I shouted, not ready for him to go yet. 'Go on then,' I said casually. 'But I'm not jumping over there.'

Luka got a small blue roll out of his jeans pocket. 'Here,' he ripped off a line of tickets. 'Be my guest.'

His fingertips brushed mine as he handed the tickets over. 'Wow,' I said, 'your hands are cold.'

Luka just looked away.

Five minutes later, I was shrieking and laughing as he smashed his dodgem car into mine. He seemed to think he was Lewis Hamilton or something, even though the cars were all peeling and rusty and falling to bits. After a while the power ran down and we both climbed out, grinning.

It was like someone had switched him on too. It made me wonder why he didn't smile more. He looked . . . nice. More than nice, and I found it hard to look at him close up again.

'Where did you get the keys to all this from, then?' I asked.

Luka didn't answer straight away and I wondered what I'd said wrong.

'My mum works . . . worked here,' he said eventually, his eyes skimming away from my face. 'In the turnstile booth mainly, taking tickets. She had lots of different jobs really, but this was the best one. She taught me how to work everything.'

'Must have been brilliant when it was open,' I said, 'getting all those free rides.'

'Yeah,' said Luka and smiled. 'Come on,' he said, 'check this out.'

He led me over to a dusty glass box. Inside there was the head and shoulders of a policeman doll. Its cheeks were painted with faded red blobs and its eyes were all starey and weird. It looked exactly like the kind of thing that would come to life in a horror movie and chop everyone to bits.

I shivered. 'What's that?'

'It's a laughing policeman,' said Luka and gave the top of the box a thump. Some tinny music started up and then the little doll began to vibrate, its hinged mouth chopping up and down.

'Hahahahahaha! Ho ho ho ho ho! Hahahahahahaha,

ho ho ho!' It went slower and slower and then stopped.

'Creepy, isn't it?' said Luka. 'Used to be terrified of that when I was a kid. Come on, I'll show you something else.'

He walked over to the ghost train with its gappy sign. The hanging plastic strips gently rippled in the wind. Luka started fiddling with an electrical box on the side and there was a painful clanking of metal as a row of cars screeched into view.

'Go on then,' he said, gesturing to the nearest one. 'Hop in.'

'What? I'm not getting in that piece of old crap!' I took a step back.

Luka did a pretend shocked face. 'I'll have you know that this was once a very fine example of a 1960s dark ride! That's what they call these things, my mum says.' He paused. 'But I didn't realise you'd be chicken.'

'It's not that,' I lied, cheeks burning. 'It just doesn't look very safe, is all.'

'What do you think's going to happen?' scoffed Luka. 'This isn't exactly Alton Towers in case you hadn't noticed. But, if you're scared of a few cardboard skeletons . . .'

I clambered into the little car and slammed down the safety bar. 'Go on, then. What are you waiting for?'

Luka pressed some more switches and the car jolted forwards again.

'*Mwhahahaha!*' said Luka in an old horror film voice. '*Prepare to enter your worst nightma-yers!* The sound effects don't work any more,' he added, normally. 'But feel free to scream.' He gave a sly grin. 'You know what they say about this fairground, don't you?'

'What?' I said, as a worm of anxiety burrowed into me.

'Haunted,' he said with a huge grin. 'People have always heard weird noises here when no one else is around.'

'Yeah, yeah, Luka,' I said. 'Just get on with it.'

The car lurched forwards and I passed between the dirty black strips.

Inside, it was dimly lit. The walls were hung with black material with tatty plastic bats stuck all over them and a dummy of Frankenstein's monster, covered in fake cobwebs, was there to greet me.

It was all about as frightening as a basket of newborn kittens.

The entrance to the next bit was shaped like those *Scream* masks you get at Halloween and the little cars trundled through the big mouth and into the next room. In this one there were lots of coffins stuck to the walls and a huge cobweb was strung across the ceiling. (That bit looked worryingly real.)

A plastic vampire in a cloak stood at one side. It only had one arm and an expression like a bad case of wind. The cars lurched forward again and swung around a corner, this time revealing a few pathetic skeletons hanging from the ceiling, one of which no longer had a head. A fake hatchet made from rubber fell out of the wall. I knew it wasn't meant to fall so far because I could see the broken wires sticking out the back. It dangled there, bouncing gently, and I started to get the proper giggles.

'Ooh, I'm so scared, Luka,' I called back to him.

The car swung around another corner, but I didn't get a chance to see what was in there because, at that moment, the car shuddered to a stop with a clanking groan and all the lights went off.

CHAPTER 7

Dark Ride

It was pitch black. The daft smile stayed on my face for a moment, even though my heart started to thrum against my ribs. This was obviously meant to be the scary bit. Well, I wasn't giving Luka the satisfaction and resolved to remain cool as a cucumber.

I folded my arms and sat back, waiting for whatever cheesiness was about to begin, determined not to be bothered.

It was very dark though . . .

The minutes ticked by. The darkness seemed to get thicker until something told me this wasn't part of the ride.

'Luka?' My voice sounded small and stupid.

I'd never been anywhere so totally dark before. I

thought darkness was just an absence of light, not something solid that presses in all around you like a giant cushion.

I breathed slowly, trying to stay calm.

This was just a technical hitch. Luka would get this daft thing moving any second and I could get back outside again.

IT WAS VERY IMPORTANT NOT TO FREAK OUT.

And then I heard something rustling behind me. I spun round.

'Hello?' I whimpered. 'Is that you, Luka? Because this isn't funny.' I was going to kill him with my bare hands when I got out of here.

The rustling, scratching noise started again, nearer now.

Maybe it was a rat.

Or maybe it was a person.

A person who wasn't Luka.

'LUKAAAAAAAAAA!' My stupid voice seemed to bounce around the walls of the enclosed space. I couldn't breathe properly. Every tiny nerve in my body felt like it was shrieking. I wanted to climb out and find my way back, but the idea of stepping on something or being grabbed was worse than staying here.

Just when I felt like I couldn't be any more frightened, something happened that made everything before seem like afternoon tea with scones and jam.

A whispering sound was seeping into the air. Then

something made a damp, flapping noise and I screamed hysterically, over and over, batting my hands around my face. Something musty and animal-like filled my nostrils. The lights snapped back on, flooding the small space with a sickly yellow glow. I leapt out of the car and legged it back the way I'd come, the vampire and the dusty old skeletons suddenly not so ridiculous any more.

I almost knocked Luka to the ground outside.

'Whatdidyoudothatfor? That wasn't funny! That (*slap*) wasn't (*slap*) funny (*slap*)!'

Luka grabbed my wrists.

'Calm down, okay!' he said. 'It only stopped for a minute! I was trying to get it going again!'

'Oh yeah?' I spat. 'So why did you creep in and scare me?'

'I did not!' His voice went all hoarse with indignation. 'A seagull got in there, didn't it? A dirty great thing. I saw it fly out.'

'Rubbish! You're just making excuses.' I sat back on my heels and tried to think.

A seagull? Could it have been just a bird?

But birds didn't whisper.

On the other hand, maybe I got a little caught up in the atmosphere and imagined the whole thing. I knew I would sound like a complete loon if I said any of this out loud. I put my damp face in my hands. I was shaking all over and about as exhausted as I'd ever felt in my whole life.

'Come on,' said Luka kindly. 'Let's go and sit down for a minute.'

We walked over to the side of the carousel and sat down on the outer rim. I took deep breaths, trying to steady myself. I really wanted to believe Luka was behind what happened but I knew I'd heard something weird in there.

'I'm really sorry,' he said. 'I didn't expect the ride to get stuck, and I really didn't come in there. It was probably just the dark playing tricks on you.' He paused and seemed to shiver. 'It does that sometimes.'

My hair was hanging down over my face. I saw Luka raise his hand and I had the crazy thought that he was going to gently brush my hair off my forehead. I stopped breathing for a moment. He let his hand drop and looked down at his feet instead.

'Yeah, well . . .' I was still shaken up and felt like I wanted to hurt him. 'Why d'you hang around in this dump anyway? Haven't you got anything better to do?'

'Not really,' said Luka in a tight voice. 'Anyway, I'm waiting.'

'Waiting? What for, a bus?'

'No,' he said. 'My mum.'

'Where's she gone?' I said, wondering if it was me who was weird or this whole conversation.

'I don't know,' said Luka quietly. 'She disappeared.'

CHAPTER 8

In the Café

The air in the café was thick with grease and sputtering steam from the big metal water heater behind the counter. I could feel sweat prickle around my hairline from the sudden heat.

I still had money from the shopping I was meant to do two days ago in my pocket. Luka said he didn't want anything but I bought him a cup of thick orange tea, which sat, untouched, in front of him. I was facing the fogged-up window, watching drops of water race towards the finishing line.

Luka hadn't said much when I suggested we got out of the fairground and found a café. He just shrugged and followed me.

I cleared my throat. 'So . . . what did you mean out

there. About your mum?'

He looked at me with those dark eyes and I wondered for a minute if he was one of those people who makes things up for attention, like Tommy Linden in my old primary school. He claimed he was JK Rowling's nephew and she'd based all the *Harry Potter* books on him.

'Just that. She's disappeared. Or been kidnapped.'

I gawped.

'Look, I know how that sounds,' he said, quietly. 'All I know is that one minute she was here, and then she was gone. I can't find any trace of her.'

I think I was probably doing a pretty good impression of a fish right then.

'She might have . . .' I didn't know how to say this nicely, '. . . just run away or something.'

Luka gave me a look like a slap. 'She'd never have gone off anywhere without me. Never.'

I stared into my hot chocolate, feeling suitably told off. 'Well, what about the police?' I said at last.

He snorted, like I'd said something really stupid. 'What about them?'

'Haven't you told them she's missing?'

Luka sighed. 'We've had a bit of history with the coppers round here. They wouldn't be interested.' He didn't say anything else.

Maybe he was one of those teenagers you hear about, with Asbos or whatever. But he didn't look like a criminal. He just looked sad.

'So where do you think she might have gone?' I said.

He ran his hands through his hair and puffed out his cheeks. 'I don't know. Just before she left, she kept whispering into the phone and hanging up when I came into the room. She was always staring off into the distance and snapping at me. Sometimes I'd hear her talking in Croatian, which she hardly ever does.'

There was another pause, then he sat up abruptly, drumming his hands hard against the table.

'Okay,' I said, trying to make sense of it all. 'When was the last time you saw her? Did she say she was going anywhere?'

Luka turned to me and gave me the strangest look then.

'What?' I said. 'Did I say something wrong?'

'No, no you didn't,' said Luka quietly. 'It's just . . .'

'Just what?'

He gave a deep sigh. 'There are . . . gaps. I can't seem to remember the last time I saw her.'

I had no idea what to say to this. Was he suffering from amnesia or something? I'd heard about a bloke who banged his head and ended up living on the streets because he'd lost his memory.

I looked around the café. A waitress with dyed blond hair piled on her head was staring at me with an odd expression. I turned back to the table.

'Luka . . .'

'What?'

'Where do you sleep?'

'Here and there. Don't worry about it.' He frowned

suddenly at something behind me. 'Why have they got that up?'

'What?' I turned round and saw he was looking at the calendar. 'What are you talking about? What's wrong with it?'

Luka's face seemed to go even paler than usual. He opened and closed his mouth, then he stood up abruptly. 'Gotta go. See you around, yeah?' He walked out of the café before I had the chance to reply.

I sat there for a few minutes, a bit dazed. I tried to imagine my mum just vanishing. Much as I sometimes wished she would, it made me shiver. Maybe Luka was mad or deluded or had lost his memory, but he was definitely lost. Like he'd been left in some dusty room like an old umbrella and someone needed to claim him.

I sighed and went to get up, then realised the waitress was watching me again.

'First sign of madness, you know,' she said.

'What is?' I said, confused.

She smiled at me. 'You drinking that?' She pointed at the cold cup of tea opposite me.

'Oh, my friend didn't want it,' I said.

'If you say so, dear,' she said and patted my hand before wiping down the table.

CHAPTER 9

Spider-Man Doesn't Use Guns

When I pushed open the front door, a small person dressed in a Spider-Man costume leapt out at me.

'Py-or, py-or!' he shouted, making gun shapes with his fingers and then, as quickly as he'd appeared, he shot up the stairs. I went towards the kitchen.

A large man with a green rugby shirt was sitting at the table. Mum was at the counter shaking biscuits onto a plate with her back to the door.

'I think it sounds very exciting,' she said, 'and it must be a good opportunity if it was worth moving from London.'

'Well, we'll see,' said the shirt in a voice that was much deeper and posher than Dad's. 'I never thought I'd come back and live in this town when I left home. The local paper wasn't exactly what I'd planned when I became a journalist! I do miss some of the buzz of working for a national. It's all dog shows and council meetings here. But . . . well, it suits me to have my mother nearby now I'm on my own.'

'Yes, I understand,' said Mum. 'It's no picnic, bringing up children alone, is it? Bel! What are you doing skulking around like that?' She went bright red.

I stared at Rugby Shirt, who seemed to fill the kitchen. He turned to me. He had blue eyes behind thick-framed glasses, a biggish nose and curly black hair.

He smiled.

I glared. 'What's going on?' I said to Mum, whose eyes swooped to the man and back to me.

'Bel, this is Will,' she said. 'He's Mrs Longmeadow's son. He came round to fix that tap for me. I mentioned to her about it being broken, and well, she said he'd come round to mend it. The tap, I mean.' Her voice trailed off and she looked so guilty and strange I could feel my heart hardening into stone with every passing second.

'This is my son, Dylan,' said Will as the tiny boy shot into the room like a red bullet. 'Or should I say, Spider-Man.'

I tried to ignore the little squirt, but it wasn't easy because he was bouncing on his dad's knees and shooting me again.

'Spider-Man doesn't use guns,' I said, rolling my eyes.

'Settle down, Dylan,' said the man poshly, but gave

50

me a look at the same time.

'Anyway, do carry on, Will,' said Mum with a cough. 'It must be such an interesting job, being a journalist. I'd love to hear more.'

The man got up, the small boy hanging over his shoulder like a wriggly sack of spuds.

'I think I'd best get off, actually,' he said. 'I'll come back round tomorrow if I may, now I know what the problem is with the tap. Mum's got some tools somewhere, I just need to dig them out. Is that okay?'

Mum pushed a strand of hair away, which had fallen in an annoyingly pretty way across her face.

'That would be marvellous, if you're sure it isn't too much trouble?'

'Not at all,' he said. 'Nice to meet you, Bel.' He held out his hand, which I shook as though it were a limp fish.

I didn't reply, but catching the eye of the little boy, I quietly stuck my tongue out at him.

Mum went to the front door with them to see them out. She still had a sickly smile on her face when she came back into the kitchen.

'*That would be marvellous, if you're sure it isn't too much trouble?*' I got the sickening whininess spot on, if I say so myself.

Mum shot me a disgusted look. 'Oh shut up, Bel,' she said, snatching the cup from the table and rinsing it under the tap as though she wanted to smash it. 'There's nothing wrong with being civil. You should try it sometime.'

I could feel my breath coming in hard bubbles. 'So

this is how it's going to be, is it?' I said. 'Now Dad's out the way?'

'Stop being so ridiculous.'

'I'm not being ridiculous,' I snapped. 'I think you fancy that Will bloke and I'm telling Dad.'

She spun round, eyes blazing at me and opened her mouth to speak. And then she stopped and just blinked. I was used to her letting off a rocket – it's just what we do, me and Mum – but this time her face was just sort of old-looking.

'Bel,' she said finally in a low voice. 'I can assure you that my only interest at the moment is getting through each day. And getting my tap mended. If I did have my eye on Will – which I don't – I very much doubt your father would care anyway.' And she swept out of the room, like *I* was the one in the wrong!

We didn't speak much for the rest of the evening.

We had our dinner on trays in the living room. It has tiny, mean windows and Mum has to put on about seventeen lamps even in the daytime so we don't crash into each other. She turned the telly onto the local news and I munched my shepherd's pie and peas miserably, thinking about my weird day and fretting about Dad not being here for Christmas. I wasn't really listening to the TV but something caught my attention.

'Work on the marina is now going full steam ahead, despite a series of initial setbacks.'

A woman with long blond hair and dark red lips was

standing in front of the patch of ground I recognised. The camera panned over her head and focused on two huge diggers. There were big fences up all around it now, but I could see the marina sign and the turrets of the fairground to the left.

'The project is already eighteen months behind schedule and running over budget,' she continued, 'but according to a spokesperson for the developer – local businessman Alexander 'Lex' McAllistair – the building work has finally begun in earnest. Phase one of the project has begun on the site of the old tile factory, which once provided work to many residents of this quiet seaside town. Phase two will start on the wasteland beyond the town centre, with plans to bring down the old Sunshine Amusement Park next spring or early summer. There was some local resistance when the fairground was first closed down.'

The screen suddenly filled with pictures of people standing on the seafront with billboards that said, *No to Marina! Save our Rides!* It didn't look like much of a protest. I wondered if Luka's mum had been one of them. I tuned back in to the newsreader. 'Lex McAllistair believes the marina project will be the making of this town.'

The man I'd seen at the Town Hall filled the screen.

'What do you say to the people who think the historic fairground should have been preserved?' asked the reporter's voice.

'Sometimes progress comes at a price,' he said solemnly.

He had a nasal sort of voice that didn't seem to go with his face. 'I grew up in this town and remember when it was a thriving seaside resort enjoyed by people from all over the South.' He gave a weighty pause. 'It hurts to see certain features of the old town go, but I believe that the Dolphin Marina project will bring Slumpton right into the twenty-first century. With a seafront to be proud of, we may once more be the jewel in the crown of the Kent Coast.'

I looked up and saw that Mum was watching him too. Getting a jibe in about one of her boyfriends being on telly was tempting, but I heroically resisted. I concentrated on eating my shepherd's pie instead.

Then I started thinking about Luka and wondered what he was having to eat that night. I pictured his dark chocolate eyes and long eyelashes again and my stomach gave a little flip. I put down my fork and pushed my half-eaten plate away.

CHAPTER 10

Checking Me Out

Next morning, once Mum had gone, I wrapped up warmly and set off for the fairground. I told myself I was going to try and find out a bit more about Luka's missing mum. It helped to keep my mind off my own problems. But deep down I knew I just wanted to see him again.

The building work was in full swing now at the marina. There were big fences up all around, just as I'd seen on telly, but I could hear the rumble of heavy machines digging from inside. There were *Keep Out* signs and warnings about wearing hard hats all over the place. One of them said, *No Hat, No Boots, No Work!* The main gate was opening to let in a digger and I stopped for a moment to let it go past. I could see a giant hole inside and loads of men like ants moving around it. Something struck me about the scene, but it was only when the gates closed again I realised what it was. Most of the workers inside looked Chinese. Odd, when I'd never seen any Chinese people around town before. And none of them seemed to have those yellow hats on, despite all the signs.

I shrugged and carried on to the fairground, slipping one of the blue tickets Luka had given me into the slot on the turnstile. *Clunk*.

I stood at the entrance for a minute. It was such a spooky place. There was a mean wind bothering rubbish that lay around the place and whistling through some of the stalls that had gaps in the hoardings. It was hard to believe there was ever music and laughter and kids charging about, lips sticky with candyfloss. I hugged myself, trying to control the shivers that were more about the atmosphere than the weather. Taking a deep breath, I set off further into the fairground.

I found him on the carousel, sitting on the lowest step, staring into space. The sight of him stopped me in my tracks – I'd never seen anyone look so alone. I could see a dirty brown sleeping bag lying next to him like a slithery skin shed by some animal. He glanced up suddenly, and a smile instantly lit up his face and made my heart do a strange backflip.

'Wotcha,' he said, springing to his feet.

'All right,' I said, suddenly feeling shy. 'What you up to?'

'Oh, you know,' he said, 'I'm just thinking things through.'

We stared at each other for a moment.

I walked over to where he was standing and sat on the edge of the carousel. He sat down too and we were silent again. He wasn't smiling any more and seemed lost in his thoughts, but it was okay all the same. I didn't feel awkward or anything with him. It felt . . . right.

After a few moments, Luka turned to look at me. 'So, you're new around here, yeah?'

I looked at him. 'How did you know that?'

He laughed. 'No one comes here any more. Well, unless they're holding a clipboard and thinking about ways to knock it all down.'

I thought about the story I'd seen on the local news. 'Luka . . .' I hesitated and he turned to look at me. Our faces were about a foot apart and I could see his eyes moving over my face and down to my lips. He was totally checking me out! I cleared my throat, hoping to stop the blush I could feel creeping up my cheeks.

'Where will you go when they pull down the fairground?' I said, or rather, squeaked.

He shrugged, trying to look unbothered. It broke the spell anyway.

'It'll be all right. I'll be sorted by then, don't you worry.'

There was an awkward silence and I thought about our weird conversation in the café.

'Had any more ideas about where your mum might have gone?' I said.

He shook his head. 'Not a clue.'

I was starting to feel a bit annoyed with him until I noticed his hands were shaking a little, which tweaked something tender inside my chest.

I did it before even thinking. I reached out and took hold of his hand. 'You're freezing, Luka.' I chafed his hand in mine the way Mum did to me sometimes. He didn't speak and for a second I thought I might actually die from the embarrassment of what I'd just done. After a few moments I dropped it, cheeks burning.

'Look,' I said. 'Have you tried having a look for any clues in the ticket booth where she worked?' I figured if I never looked him directly in the eye again, I might survive this excruciating moment.

'Well, it wasn't exactly an office,' he said in a husky sort of voice.

'No,' I said, 'but she probably spent tons of time in there.'

'Hmm,' said Luka, all normal again. 'You might have said something sensible. I bet that doesn't happen very often.'

'Don't push your luck!' I said, relief flooding through me that I hadn't frightened him away with the whole hand-rubbing thing.

We set off towards the ticket booth, both of us grinning.

CHAPTER 11

Picture Perfect

A door was cut into the back of the booth. Luka gave it a shove. It didn't move. He took the bunch of keys from his pocket and found the right one. I followed him inside.

It was just big enough for us both to squeeze inside. There was a shelf running right the way round and a swivel chair. A thin layer of dust blurred every surface and bandy-legged spiders covered the flaking paint.

The window of the booth had a hole in the middle, cracks fanning out from it in delicate patterns. There was a nasty smell in the background and my nose led my eyes towards an old yoghurt pot on the side, the spoon now sticking up out of furry green mould.

I turned round and then gasped.

Luka grinned. 'What do you think? Good, aren't they?' he said with obvious pride.

I moved closer to the back of the door. It was completely covered with photographs. Many of them were of the fairground. There were close-ups of the wooden horses on the carousel, pictures of rows of candyfloss and several showing the rides in motion. The blurry colours and lights almost made me dizzy. Others were of people's faces – looks of fear or excitement as people queued up for rides, one of an old lady with broken teeth beaming into the camera and clutching a teddy. Some of them, near the bottom, were taken at strange angles on the rides. One was inside a hall of mirrors so you could see someone standing with a camera, presumably Luka's mum. Her feet were neatly together and she looked small and delicate. There were a whole bunch of black weird ones from inside the ghost train that didn't seem to be of anything much. Around the edges were some pictures of the sea that were moody and dark, like paintings.

'They're amazing.'

'Eva was really into photography. She'd sometimes go off for a whole day taking pictures. Used to dream of having an exhibition some day.'

There was a silence and I had the weirdest sensation that Luka wasn't in the room with me any more.

'Is this her?'

In the top corner was a strip of pictures from a photo booth. The woman had a purple woolly hat pulled over long dark hair and brown eyes which were just like Luka's, except hers were full of mischief. She was pressing her cheek next to a mini Luka, who was grinning into the lens and showing off a gap in his front teeth.

'She's really pretty,' I said quietly.

'Yeah,' said Luka with a sigh, 'everyone says that. She's loads of fun too. Bit mad though. Usually in a good way. Like, she'll wake up one morning and say, "Come on, give school a miss today", because she fancies a day out together. And she never nags me about stuff, like most mums. But sometimes she gets sad and drinks too much wine and goes to bed for a day or so. I sort of thought she was headed that way before all this happened.'

'You called her Eva just then,' I began and Luka shrugged, understanding my question.

'She says it makes her feel old to be called "Mum" so I sometimes call her by her name. She was only twenty when I was born. She's more like a big sister to me than a mother, really. We moved about a fair bit before coming here when I was twelve and we had to look after each other. She always used to say it was me and her against the world.'

I let this sink in. So Luka wasn't really from Slumpton either. Maybe that was partly why I liked him so much.

'Were you born in Croatia?'

'Yeah,' said Luka, 'but we came to the UK when I was one so I don't remember anything about it. And Eva never keeps up any traditions or anything. Says she was glad to see the back of her old life. She left my dad because he knocked her about. She loved . . . um . . . loves it here.'

I noticed he'd used past tense and a look of pain flickered across his face before he spoke again. Maybe something really bad had happened to Eva. For a minute I felt as though he was alone in his thoughts. Then he gave himself a little shake. 'C'mon, I'm freezing my balls off in here. Let's start searching. You start that side and I'll do over here.'

We both ran our hands along the shelf underneath the counter. I found nothing but dust and crusty flies, which I quickly brushed onto the floor with a shudder. I looked around the small space and met Luka's eye. He'd found nothing either. Then I noticed that there was a gap in the bottom part of the old-fashioned till. It was too narrow to put my fingers into, but when I crouched down and peered inside, I could see some paper in there. I looked around and found an old knife sitting on the window sill with some tacks and a few pennies. Gently pushing it inside the gap, I jiggled it about. At first, it just pushed everything further inside and I cursed quietly. Then I managed to get it to bring the papers to the front. Luka pulled them out and started looking at them.

'Bill, bill, library fine, bill . . . Oh, hang on, what's this?' He held up a sheet of notepaper.

On it was some swirly handwriting in blue biro. It said, *Manley Road flats awaiting demolition. Could hold up to 50.* Underneath were lists of numbers, which looked like times from a twenty-four hour clock. Lots were circled and some were marked *Dover*, some *Folkestone* and some *Harwich*.

We looked at each other. Then another piece of paper caught my eye – a plain black and white flyer *TMS Knitwear*, it said. *Quality Fashions at Wholesale Prices*. There was an address. On the bottom of the piece of paper were two words, handwritten and underlined: *Contact Bluebird?*

Luka traced the words with his finger. 'That's her writing, that bit there.'

I opened my mouth to speak but he grabbed my arm and put his finger to my lips, eyes wide.

Seconds later I heard it too. Male voices coming nearer.

Luka pushed the top of my head down and we both folded onto our knees. I was squashed right up against him in the small space. For a second I was distracted by how nice it felt to be close to him, before being scared took over.

The men got closer. One was speaking in a harsh-sounding foreign accent, but one word – 'Lex' – kept standing out. I very slowly raised myself up so I could peek out and could just make out a couple of thickset blokes, both with woolly hats pulled low over their brows. One of them looked up and I realised it was the no-neck one again, who I'd seen at the Town Hall and at the marina. I realised something was on the ground and gasped. It was a man with black hair, curled into a foetal position.

Luka pulled me down and put his arm gently around

my shoulder. I was glad he did because the next unmistakable sounds were grunts of pain. I somehow knew the man was being kicked. Tears swelled in my throat. I was shaking all over and I could feel Luka flinching at the sound of every blow. It was horrible, horrible. Finally, I heard the man speaking again, sounding out of breath and I shrugged off Luka's protecting hand to peek again.

The injured man was being held up by the armpits and had blood running down his face. He looked Indian or Pakistani from what I could make out. His eyes were open and unfocused but at least he was alive.

Luka pulled me down again, harder this time, and his eyes were angry, but also scared.

The voices started to recede and we heard the metal clang of the gates closing.

Luka lifted himself up to peek over the top of the ledge. 'Coast's clear,' he said, in a wobbly way. The small space was suddenly unbearable and we elbowed each other in our haste to get out.

I couldn't seem to get air properly into my lungs and bent over. I felt a tentative hand on my back.

'Are you okay?' said Luka gently, and I nodded, swallowing back the urge to throw up. I stood up straight on my shaking legs and we stared at each other.

I couldn't believe what I'd just heard. I'd lived in the capital city all my life and the only crime I'd known was when someone pranged Mum's car and drove off. But the minute I move to a sleepy seaside town, it was all disappearing mothers and people being beaten in abandoned fairgrounds.

'Who do you think those men were?' I said, when I trusted myself to speak.

'I don't know,' said Luka. He was looking queasy too, his face pale. 'I've never seen them before.'

'Do you think your mum —?' I started to say but Luka cut me off.

'Eva didn't mix with people like that! Everyone round here blames immigrants for everything, but it's families who've lived here all their lives that are the worst.'

I tried to speak but he hadn't finished.

'She'd never be that stupid. You're as bad as the police. Just because she works in a fairground and looks a bit Romany. You think she's not a decent person.'

'I don't think that!' I felt tears stinging my eyes again and swiped my hand across them.

'Well, plenty do in this town.'

We stood there miserably, in silence.

'We should tell the police about what we saw,' I said.

'What are you going to say, Bel? We don't know who they are. We shouldn't even be in here.'

I didn't really need much persuading. Suddenly I noticed something.

'Luka! Your hand!'

He looked down. A big shard of glass was sticking into the fleshy part of his palm. He must have leaned on it inside the booth. I reached towards him to help and he spun away from me.

'Luka, let me help!'

'Leave it, I'll sort it out,' he said in a panicky voice. 'It's all right. I'll deal with it. You'd better go. Your mum will be worried.' He kept his hand turned away from me and pulled out the glass.

'You might need stitches!' I yelped.

'I'm FINE!' he said. 'Just leave it!'

I turned away. Suddenly I just wanted to be home and away from all this bad stuff and Luka's stupid pride.

'Hey!' he called.

'What?' I said a bit shortly.

'Will you come back?'

The desperation in his eyes made me hesitate, but I was angry and shaken up and wanted to be away. 'I don't know, Luka,' I said. 'Maybe.'

He turned away and I was already starting to feel bad. His voice was crisp. 'Okay, well . . . see you.'

'Yeah,' I said. 'See you.'

CHAPTER 12

Is That You, Babe?

The lights were all on when I got back and I could hear quiet laughter from upstairs.

'Mum?'

I took off my coat and slung it over the banister before peering up the stairs. Mum's head bobbed over the top and she put a finger to her lips.

'Shhh! The little one's asleep on my bed,' she hissed and promptly disappeared again.

Little one? Little what?

I clomped up the stairs. I didn't need any more surprises after the day I'd had.

Mum and that Will bloke were squeezed into the tiny bathroom. He was holding a broken tap in his hand, looking sheepish. He nodded at me and I ignored him.

'What's going on?' I said, sounding like a forty-year-old schoolteacher. I realised these were the exact words I'd spoken last time I'd seen them together.

Mum was all pink and twinkly.

'Will was helping with the tap, but it seems to be in a worse state than we thought,' she said, sounding supremely unbothered.

'I'm not exactly a DIY whizz, in truth,' said Will apologetically. 'Look, I could run over to B&Q, but I don't want to choose the wrong style of tap, and there's Dylan. Mum's at the doctor, or I'd ask her to watch him for a bit.'

Mum's gaze bounced to me and then back to Will again.

'Unless . . .' he began and she nodded encouragingly. 'Unless Bel wouldn't mind keeping an ear out for half an hour. Mum will be back soon. You could come with me then and choose the design you like.'

I was just about to open my mouth when Mum said, 'Good idea! You're old enough to do this now, Bel. We won't be long.'

Before I'd even had time to scrape my eyebrows back into their proper position, they were bundling down the stairs and into coats.

'Will Dylan sleep for long?' said Mum, turning to Will, glowing like she was looking into the sun.

'Should be out for ages,' said Will, 'but if he wakes up, maybe you could just tell him where we are and put the telly on for him?'

'Fine,' I said, feeling like I was spitting out stones and

not words. 'No problem. Off you go. Have a completely fabulous time.'

Honestly, they couldn't get out that door fast enough. So I'm an unpaid babysitter now, I thought. They might be choosing a tap, but by the look on Mum's face, it could just as well have been a candle-lit dinner for two.

Poor Dad. It wasn't right. I would be giving him a full report when I saw him, for sure.

I poured myself some juice and sat down at the kitchen table, resting my head in my hands and making a curtain of my hair over my face. I almost didn't have the energy to be angry with Mum.

It really had been a horrible, freaky day. I wanted to tell Mum, but knew if I did, she wouldn't let me out the door again until I was at least thirty.

'Where's my daddy?'

The reedy little voice made me jump. Dylan was standing in the doorway, hair sticking up, face puffy and a scraggy toy dog dangling from his hand.

Oh dear.

'He's just popped out with my mum,' I said, trying to sound cheerful, but I think I was baring my teeth – his eyes got more circular.

Never having had a brother or sister, I didn't really know what to do with small kids. I mean, obviously I was one once, but I didn't have that many friends when I was little. Mum says I was bossy and put people off, which was obviously a total lie.

I know Mum and Dad wanted me to have a brother

or sister, but I think Mum had some sort of medical problem. Then, last year, she'd finally got pregnant.

It wasn't long after Nan died. Mum and Dad had been so happy, despite Mum being sad about Nan and barfing all the time. And then one day I got home from school and Mum's friend Lynne was there. She bundled me into the kitchen and told me that Mum had lost the baby. For a moment I didn't understand and wanted to say, 'Lost it where?' but kept my gob shut for once. She was sleeping upstairs and I wasn't to disturb her. For some reason they couldn't get hold of Dad and it was late when he got back. I heard them rowing and Mum crying, then the door slamming.

Anyway.

So I know nothing about small kids. Just as long as he didn't start crying it would all be fine.

'Oh . . . What's the matter, Dylan?'

His face had scrunched up and although he wasn't making any sound, tears were definitely imminent.

'Don't want you, stinky girl!' He started to wail then at ear-splitting volume. 'Want my daddy!'

I made shushy flapping movements with my hands, which only made him screech louder.

'Hey, we've got crisps!' I said desperately. 'Do you like crisps, Dylan?' Everyone likes crisps. He stopped wailing and gave a huge hiccup, before nodding suspiciously. I tried not to look at the slimy green trail dangling from his nose to his top lip as I went over to the cupboard and dug about to find the Unhappy

Shopper Crappy Crisps Mum bought these days.

A few moments later, the kitchen was filled with hard munching. I had to keep my eyes away from his bogey trail, but I was starving because I hadn't eaten since breakfast. I decided a second packet was probably in order.

Dylan was swinging his feet backwards and forwards, his blue spotted socks hanging off the end and making his feet look about twice as long as they were. For some reason this seemed funny. We eyed each other as we ate our crisps. No one spoke.

It reminded me of when two gunslingers squared up to each other in old cowboy films and that music came into my head. I found myself pretending to pull a gun and aimed my crisp at him. He chortled, spraying cheese and onion shards across the table. He was quite cute when he smiled, despite all the grot on his face.

Not needing any more encouragement, he leapt up and started firing off shots with his fingers. I dived under the table, pulling the plastic tablecloth down to hide my face. He giggled like a mad thing and I could feel laughter rising inside me like froth as he ducked down and pointed his grinning face under the table.

Dylan shot out and ran into the living room. I got up from under the table and followed him. He was sitting under a pile of cushions on the sofa, his small feet poking out in a very obvious way.

'Where can he be?' I said in a loud, fakey voice and started to pull off the cushions slowly. The whole sofa was almost vibrating with his silent chuckles now and just as I got to the last one, he burst out like a cannonball, yelling at the top of his voice and charged up the stairs. I was getting a bit bored with this game now, to be honest, so I went back into the kitchen, wondering how long Mum and whatsisface were going to be.

The phone rang and I picked it up.

'Steve?' said a woman's voice. 'Is that you, babe?'

'Who is this?' I said.

'Oh, I'm sorry,' the woman sounded flustered. 'He left his phone and I was ringing last number called because I thought he was . . .'

Icy water seemed to rush through me and I slammed the phone down. Why was some woman ringing here and asking for Dad? And calling him *babe*?

It had to be a mistake. A wrong number. Steve wasn't such an unusual name, was it?

Dylan, sensing the change in the atmosphere, came into the kitchen with his thumb in his mouth, his eyes wide.

'Dylan, do you want to watch some telly now?' I said shakily. To my relief he nodded.

I got on the sofa next to him and he shuffled his small, hot body next to me. It was weirdly comforting. We watched *Spongebob Squarepants* for a bit and I must have dropped off, because the next thing I knew, Mum and Will were smiling in the doorway of the living room. Dylan had his head on my lap, curled like a little prawn.

'Everything been okay?' she said.

'Fine.' I got up, hastily, making Dylan flop sideways.

He sat up, looking bewildered. I didn't want Mum entertaining ideas of me gaining a step-brother, however cute he was.

After dinner, I was curled up on the sofa thinking about everything that had happened earlier. I'd witnessed something horrible but I couldn't stop going over the moment when we were sat together on the carousel. I caught my breath when I remembered the way Luka looked at me. For a crazy moment I'd actually thought he might be going to kiss me. The more likely explanation was that hanging around in that weird place was making my imagination do mad things.

Mum came into the room with a big B&Q bag. She was grinning a nervous sort of grin. 'Hey, lazybones,' she said. 'How about getting off your bum and giving me a hand?'

She really had no idea how hard a day I'd had, but I swung my legs round and sat up. She pulled a large box out of the bag.

'What's that?' I said, even though the words *4.5 feet Spruce Pine Artificial Tree* were clearly written in big letters on the side of the box.

'It's a Christmas tree,' said Mum, her smile faltering. 'Thought it was about time we made this house a bit more homely. We can decorate it together. Look, I even bought some —'

'But it's fake!' I cut across her. 'We always have a real tree.'

73

Mum had been hanging some tinsel around her neck and her arms fell to her sides.

'I know that,' she said patiently, 'but we haven't got the space now and this one will last for ever. Look, it's quite nice! Very realistic, in fact.' She pulled the green plasticky thing out of the box and set about getting it upright.

It did look realistic. You'd never have known it was fake if you had no sense of smell and no soul. It just wasn't Christmas with a fake tree.

My eyes started to fill up. In that moment I'd have done anything to have a time machine that could take me back to London and my old life, with Dad there. Even if they were fighting, life there was better than this grotty place with scary men and lonely boys with lost eyes and mothers who didn't even seem to care that they had killed Christmas stone dead.

Mum was staring at me. 'Bel? What is it?' She crawled over on her knees and I burst out crying. I just couldn't stop it. Snot and tears were all down my face but she put her arms around me anyway. I wailed like a baby.

'Oh Bel,' she said softly, stroking my hair. 'I know it's been hard for you, moving here. And I know how much you're missing your dad. But we'll get used to it. It'll be brilliant in the summer, being by the sea. Everything will be okay, honey, it really will.'

I stopped crying and took my hands away from my face. I knew my eyes had almost disappeared and my nose was still running but I didn't care. 'You've got to make Dad come for Christmas!'

She frowned. 'Bel, it's not as straightforward —'

'You have to!' I interrupted. 'If you tell him you want him here too, he'll come, I know he will.'

Mum sat back on her heels and studied my face for a long time. When she spoke again her voice was very quiet. 'I know that you think this is all down to me. But there are complicated things I can't really explain to you, grown-up things, and —'

'You made him go, so don't pretend you didn't!'

Sometimes I find myself standing and shouting and can't remember exactly how I got there. This was one of those times.

'I know that's what happened! It's all your fault!'

Mum's face hardened as she got to her feet too. 'Bel, you know nothing about it.'

'Then tell me then!' I wailed.

Mum looked at me for a long, long time. When she spoke her voice was shaky. 'It's over between me and your dad, Bel,' she said quietly. 'We're not going to be living here all together. You have to face that. The truth is that me and your dad, well, we've moved on. I'm sorry, but that's just the way it is.'

'LIAR!' I screamed. I was so close I could see my crazed reflection in her eyes. 'It's all your fault! You're a liar and I hate you! I hate you!'

I felt the slap before my brain registered what had happened.

Mum gasped, like she couldn't believe what she'd done. 'Bel, wait!' she shouted.

But I turned away and walked out of the room with as much dignity as I could muster. As I was leaving, I heard the Christmas tree slump sideways with a sound like a sigh.

CHAPTER 13

Runaway

My bedroom door had an old-fashioned lock and key.

I took great satisfaction in hearing Mum wiggle the handle desperately. I didn't go downstairs for the rest of the evening, just lay in bed snuffling until I could barely see through my puffy eyes.

I must have slept eventually because soon weak light was coming through my curtains and Mum was calling through my bedroom door.

'Bel? Bel, are you awake?' She rattled the handle. 'Look, darling . . . I'm so sorry I . . . I slapped you. I will never, ever do it again, I promise. Bel?'

I ignored her and put my hands over my ears until I made out the muffled thump of the front door closing. I wasn't prepared to hear any more of her poisonous lies.

Lying there in the unfriendly, empty house, I'd never felt so lonely. It was like there was nowhere I really belonged any more. I thought about going back to the fairground, which was about the only place I'd felt like me lately, despite all the strangeness. I wanted to see Luka, badly. But then I remembered the way we'd parted. Maybe he wouldn't be pleased to see me and I didn't think I could bear it if he told me to get lost. I was so sore inside already.

The only place I could imagine being was back in London, at Jasmine's house. We'd always been able to make each other feel better about stuff. Within ten minutes I was stuffing clothes into my rucksack, trying to work out how long it would take to walk to the station and find a train back to London. I decided I'd ring Jasmine from the train. Or better still, surprise her.

I slowed down as I got to the end of the road and patted my pocket. There was forty pounds in there, saved from my birthday. I'd had an idea of saving up for an iPod, but that seemed stupid now. What use was an iPod when your family was in bits and your own mother hit you?

It was freezing today and my teeth were chattering a bit as I hurried along the road.

I walked for about fifteen minutes in the direction I thought I'd find the station. It was definitely around here somewhere . . . maybe around the next corner. Or maybe just a bit further.

After a while I slowed down as the horrible realisation sunk in.

I'd somehow managed to get lost in this tiny, poxy town.

I stopped walking and let the rucksack fall to the ground, narrowly missing a clump of dog poo. I looked around at the quiet street and sighed heavily, leaning against a wall.

I put my head in my hands and tried to picture myself getting off the train at St Pancras station. I imagined all the busy, purposeful people stampeding past me. What did I really think would happen if I ran away? Jasmine's mum would probably get straight on the phone to Mum the minute she saw me. I pushed myself away from the wall, heart like a brick. I decided I'd just go home and wrap myself in a duvet, eat biscuits and watch daytime TV. Maybe I could blank out the world for a while.

I didn't have the energy to walk and dragged my weary bones to the nearest bus stop to check out where I was. Two women with buggies were waiting there and chatting. I must have looked a bit starey-eyed and mad because they shifted along slightly.

'Can I get a bus back into town from here?' I said, and one of them nodded.

'Should be just a few minutes,' she said.

'Thanks,' I mumbled and perched on the end of the bench.

The two women carried on their conversation, which cut into my numb thoughts.

'I heard it wasn't coming down for another six months,' said one.

'Seems they've brought the schedule forward,' said the other woman. 'My cousin knows someone who works for McAllistair. It's going at the end of January.'

'Sooner they do it, the better,' said the first woman. 'That fairground is an eyesore, if you ask me. You know what they say about it, don't you?'

The other woman snorted. 'I can't believe you'd fall for that nonsense!'

'People hear things though! And how do you explain the fact that there are sometimes lights in there?'

'I tell you, if that old dump is haunted, then I'm Lady Gaga!' said the other woman. They both burst out laughing.

My thoughts were churning around my head like clothes in a tumble dryer.

Hardly surprising that the fairground had a weird reputation. But I was more worried about the other thing they'd said. Luka wouldn't know that he only had a month left to live in the fairground. I pictured a huge pile of rubble. What would happen to him then? Maybe he'd leave Slumpton and move on somewhere else to look for Eva. The thought of never seeing him again was suddenly so awful I sank back against the hard plastic seat in a way that made the two mothers stare at me. I had to see him again, even if he was funny with me after yesterday.

The bus appeared and the doors opened with a loud hiss. The women clambered on with all their stuff but I just stood there.

'You getting on or what?' said the driver.

'Do you go anywhere near Sunshine Park?' I asked.

The driver nodded. 'Get a move on, if you're coming.'

I used one of my tickets to get through the gates. I shivered as I looked around, thinking about the violence we'd witnessed yesterday. I felt a spasm of guilt about not going to the police. I'd pounced on what Luka had said because I was scared, but it wasn't right to let something like that happen and not be reported, was it?

I was getting colder and colder standing there so I decided to just put one foot in front of the other until I found Luka.

I walked further into the fairground, but I only found his sleeping bag by the carousel. I bent down and touched the thin, shiny material.

The wind whistling through all the boarded-up places made the back of my neck prickle but I forced myself to go on, trying not to look at the ghost train.

Before long, the entrance to the old rollercoaster soared above me. It looked about four hundred years old. I shivered at the thought of rattling along in the rusty-looking carriages. Dad would have been on there like a shot. He thought I loved these rides too, but secretly I'd rather have stayed with Mum down on the ground and eaten candyfloss. Not that I was ever going to admit it.

Towards the back of the fairground there was a low row of stalls with a roof and shutters along the front. A flaky sign on the roof read, *Munch Zone* and there was a picture of a huge open mouth with a big red tongue. It made me feel as though the mouth wanted to eat me too. There was something about this place that just blew up fears like a big magnifying glass.

At that moment, I heard a noise and spun round.

Luka was sitting up high on the side of the rollercoaster staring straight ahead. I couldn't read his face at all. He looked like he'd been there for ages. Suddenly he got up and started to climb further up the metal struts. My heart began to thud as I ran over. He glanced down, but it was like he didn't see me at all.

'What are you doing? Come down, Luka! You'll get hurt!' I shouted. But he just carried on climbing. A big gust of wind blew a sheet of cardboard into the air and it whooshed towards Luka. I screamed. He batted it away but slipped, so that he ended up on his knees on the narrow ledge.

'Luka!' I was scared to breathe, as though I might somehow make him fall and I was shaking hard now with fear as I watched him heave himself upright again. He looked down at me finally, the wind pushing his black hair back from his face in a fan.

'What are you doing?' I screamed.

He said something back but the wind just whisked it away.

'What did you say?'

'I've been figuring some things out,' he yelled. 'I have to *know*. I'm sorry, Bel.'

And then he started to climb higher. I shouted until my throat ached. I wondered if I should run back to the seafront to find help, but I couldn't bear to move in case it was just my willpower alone that was keeping him from falling.

Soon he'd got to the top of the first support. There was a flat ledge and I gasped with relief that he was standing on something solid.

Then he did the worst thing I've ever seen. He closed his eyes, put his arms out to the sides . . . and stepped off the edge into thin air.

CHAPTER 14

You've Got to Help Me

'Luka!'

I covered my face because I couldn't bear to see it but I still heard the sound he made as he hit the ground. I opened my eyes and ran over. He was facing away from me, lying on his stomach, his arm at an awkward angle. He looked very still and I fell down onto my knees next to him, crying in big, wracking sobs. His eyes were open but glassy-looking and his cheek was pressed hard against the ground.

'You're going to be OK, Luka!' I wailed. 'I'm going to get help. Just stay still.'

I took off my jacket and laid it over his shoulders. I

bent down and kissed his cold, dirty cheek. Then I ran faster than ever in my life towards the exit turnstile. The only person outside was a woman pushing a pram along the road. She looked alarmed as I ran up to her.

'You've got to help me!' I screamed. 'It's my friend! He's had an accident!'

She jiggled the pram as the baby inside started to wail. 'Where?'

'He's in there!' I pointed to the fairground and the woman pulled a pink mobile phone from her pocket.

She made the call, darting suspicious glances at me the whole time. 'They said they'd be here soon,' she said when she'd hung up. She patted me awkwardly on the arm. 'You know you shouldn't be in there, don't you? It's dangerous.'

I just hung my head and cried quietly, wondering if there was anything they could do or if Luka was already dead.

It seemed like no time before a big yellow and green ambulance with all its nee-nawing and lights screeched up next to us. A man and a woman in paramedic gear leapt out, radio noises crackling in the background.

'Where's the casualty?' said the woman to me.

'He's in there,' I said and the two paramedics exchanged glances. They were looking at me differently now, as though I was some kind of vandal.

'Look,' said the woman, 'it's going to be very hard to get the rig in there. Take me to your friend and we can work out how we can help him, okay?'

I nodded miserably and the lady paramedic came with me through the gates using the tickets.

'What were you doing in here anyway?' she said, not unkindly as we hurried through the fairground, past all the boarded-up stalls. 'Didn't you see all those signs?'

I just snivelled.

'Tell me exactly what happened,' she said.

'It's my friend,' I said. 'He climbed up the side of the rollercoaster. Then he just threw himself off!'

'Is he conscious?'

'I don't know,' I said. 'He's just lying there. He's right around this corner.'

We came towards the concession stands.

'He's just over . . .'

The words died in my throat.

'Where?' said the paramedic.

I rushed over to the spot and saw that my jacket had been slung over the bottom rail of the rollercoaster. I opened and closed my mouth a few times.

'But what, where . . . ?' I ran around wildly, trying to see where he'd gone. 'Luka!' I yelled at the top of my voice. 'Where are you? You need help!'

The paramedic started to speak into her radio. 'Are you sure he was hurt?' she said, turning to me. Her words were sharp but her eyes were kinder. 'You know that wasting our time stops us from helping people who really need us.'

'I'm sorry!' I wailed. 'But my friend really was here!'

Her face softened. 'Look, I'm sure if he was able to run

away then he's just a bit shaken up. I'll put a call in just in case he turns up at A&E, but I'm sure he's fine.'

She carried on speaking but I wasn't listening any more. None of it made sense. We came back through the gates and I mumbled that I was sorry again and walked quickly away.

I felt like I could hear the crackling radio all the way home.

CHAPTER 15

Lockett's Rise

It was 22 December, but there was no Christmas cheer in our house. Every time Mum tried to have that 'proper talk' with me, I walked off. So we passed each other like strangers, mouths set into lines.

But I wasn't even thinking about the row any more. I couldn't stop going over and over the pictures in my head of what had happened with Luka. Maybe I'd misjudged how far he fell? Then I remembered the awkward way he was lying. He must have been really badly hurt, he *must* have been. How could he have got up and walked away? I kept imagining him lying injured somewhere and I couldn't bear it. Mum was at work, so I decided to look in the fairground again, just in case he'd come back.

I grabbed my jacket from the cupboard and put it on.

My fingers closed around some paper in one of the pockets. It was an old envelope, folded into squares and then folded again. I opened it out, the creases like veins across the scrunched paper. The address read:

Ms Eva Novak
53 Lockett's Rise
Seaforth Road
Slumpton
LM26 6RY

Eva? It hit me. Luka's mum. He must have put this in my pocket after the fall. It was obviously a message. He wanted me to find him.

I wasn't taking any chances this time and rooted about in a drawer for the map of the town Mum had bought when we moved in. I stuffed it into my pocket before heading out.

It was so cold the air hurt my lungs, but the sky was blue as a summer's day as I trudged up the steep hill behind our houses.

It didn't take long to find the beginning of Lockett's Rise.

I don't know why, but my heart started to bang against my chest like a trapped bird and the back of my neck prickled as I got further up the road.

47, 49, 51 . . .

Number 53 had a neglected air. There were hanging baskets with dried brown stuff hanging out and the windows were dirty. I peered inside and could see a small kitchen with just a table and a few chairs. It felt like no one had lived here for a long time. Could this be the wrong house? I fumbled for the envelope, but no, it definitely said number 53.

I heard a noise and noticed a round, pink face at the window next door, two bright eyes looking at me. Before I could turn away, an old lady was out the front, her arms crossed over her chest and her chin raised.

'Can I help you, dear?' she said.

'Urgh.' Better try again. I cleared my throat and tried to speak like a normal person. 'Have you seen the boy who lived here?'

The old lady stared at me for ages and a horrible feeling began to curdle in my stomach.

'Oh dear,' she said at last, her hand fluttering to her chest. 'Hasn't anyone told you?'

'Told me what?' I whispered. I had a horrible premonition that I didn't want to know the answer.

'I think you'd better come inside.'

'No!' I didn't mean to say it like that and the lady flinched. 'Sorry, but can you just tell me? Have you seen him?'

'Oh dear,' she said again. 'Oh dear . . . Well, the thing is, lovey, I'm afraid he, he passed away.'

I had a rushing feeling in my ears and a big hot wave of sick in my throat.

Tears splintered everything at the thought of Luka crawling away from his fall and dying alone.

The old lady was speaking again but my brain wasn't able to untangle what she was saying.

'What?' I squeaked.

'It was a dreadful thing,' she said. 'As it's the anniversary coming up, I was just thinking about it.'

What was she talking about? 'What do you mean, *anniversary*?'

She hesitated again. 'Well . . . it's almost a year since the boy and his mother died.'

Grey pavement rushed towards me like a wall.

A strong grip was on my arm and then a hallway smelt of furniture polish.

A sofa with patterns and wallpaper with different patterns swam in front of me, so that they all mixed together and made the sick in my throat keep rising until it blurted out of my mouth, right into a basin that was magically in front of me.

I sat there, too numb to think straight and she was back, removing the stinky basin without a word, and then putting down a tray with a teapot and a plate of ginger biscuits. The room was silent apart from the sound of a clock ticking and completely wrong, cheerful radio noises from another room.

The old lady handed me a cup of milky tea and I took a sip, my hands shaking so much I slopped some on my jeans.

'Lots of sugar,' she said. 'That's what you need for shock. Have a biscuit too.'

I didn't want one but took one like a robot and bit into it. The taste seemed to bring everything back into focus along with a bright thudding in my chest.

'Did you know him well, lovey?' The old lady had

her head on one side like a bird.

I just nodded. Protests were screaming inside my head. *It's obviously a mistake! How can he be dead when I've spent half the week with him? You've got it wrong, that's all. It's just a stupid mistake.*

But the words didn't come. I just sat there, while she talked quietly.

'It was an awful thing. There was an accident, a car accident. The police said she lost control of the vehicle and they drove straight off St Lawrence's Headland into the sea.'

I was staring at her, still unable to take in her words.

'They said they . . .' she hesitated, '. . . died instantly.' She cleared her throat.

I got up abruptly. 'I have to go now.' My voice was hoarse and every part of me was hurting like someone had punched me all over.

She got up too and placed her warm, dry hand on mine. 'I know it's a shock. But time is a great healer and you're still young. You'll get over this, really you will.'

I pulled my hand away and walked out of the room. I didn't even thank her for being so kind to me. I just had to be alone. As I walked out of the front door and back down the road, I could feel her concerned eyes boring into my back.

It couldn't possibly be true. It was too crazy to be true.

But maybe it *was* true? Maybe it had been right in front of my nose all along and I'd just been too dumb to see it.

No one could have fallen from that height and walked away. He wouldn't let me see his hand when he cut it on the glass either. I thought of the waitress in the café, looking at me so weirdly. She must have thought I was cracked, sitting there talking to myself.

I've been figuring some things out, Bel. That's what he said, right before he jumped.

I knew exactly where to look, but when I got to the outside of the fairground, everything was different. There were vans parked all over the place. A big green portakabin was in pieces on the side of the road. I stood there, unsure what to do next when a low whistle came from nearby. I looked over and saw there was another old building with a tatty yard behind it. I slipped through a gap in the fence and there was Luka, sitting on a wall.

He looked like he'd been waiting for ages. We didn't speak. All I could do was stare at his face and neck and hands which looked so real and fleshy, and his trainers and jeans and hoodie. Just like any other boy. There was the hole in the knee of his jeans where you could even see a circle of pink skin. I remembered touching his cheek and how cold he was. But *real*.

'Go on then.'

When he spoke it made me jump. 'Go on then, what?'

'Get all the questions you're gagging to ask out the way.'

'Is it . . . is it true?'

He shrugged. 'Seems so, doesn't it?'

'But you're so . . . solid.' We stared at each other again

93

and then I had a mad notion. 'Is this some sort of stupid joke, Luka, because if it is . . .' My voice went into a squeak.

He did a disgusted swoop with his eyes. 'It's not looking very funny to me,' he said. 'I didn't know until yesterday either. It was seeing the date on that calendar in the café. It made a bunch of weird things make sense.'

'Can everyone see you?'

'No. Just you.'

'Why me?'

'Don't know. No idea. Next?'

'Where do you go at night? Do you sleep?'

He gave me such a look then, my insides withered a bit. 'Of course I sleep. I've been sleeping rough in the fairground. You knew that.'

'What about eating? Can you eat like other people?'

He looked up at the sky. 'Probably. But I can't remember being hungry or thirsty.'

I hesitated before speaking again. 'Can you, you know, do stuff?' He gave me a withering look and I instantly regretted it.

'Stuff?'

'Like, I don't know, walking through walls.'

He got up, his expression icy. 'Let's see, shall we?'

And then to my horror, he ran full-pelt into the wall.

I screamed as he thumped into it and staggered back, clutching his head. But there was no mark and he seemed to recover quickly.

'Doesn't look like it, does it?' he said, a bit out of breath.

I knew I should stop but I had one more question. It was the hardest of all to get out.

'What does it . . . feel like?'

'What, being dead?'

I flinched.

'It's a laugh-a-minute, what do you think?' He spat the words out like hard pips. 'You feel so lonely it's like someone has scooped out your insides. Like you're the only person in the world. It feels like a bad joke and everyone is in another room laughing. Any minute now someone will say, "Surprise!" and everything will be normal again.' He was breathing heavily. He sank back against the wall. When he spoke again he sounded sort of hollow. 'That's how it feels.'

'Do you remember anything?' I said and he shook his head, his eyes fearful. I took a deep breath, knowing I was about to hurt him.

'Luka, I'd better tell you some stuff,' I said quietly.

Chapter 16

Knowing

It was the hardest thing I'd ever had to do. As I told him what the old lady had said, his eyes were sort of pleading, like he didn't want to hear the words, but when I did hesitate, he hurried me on.

I finished speaking and reached for his hand. He gripped mine so hard it hurt.

'I dream about being trapped. I can hear Eva's voice calling to me but I can't reach her.' He stared at the ground. Then he said, 'So she's dead too?' as though it had suddenly just hit him.

He jumped to his feet, and squeezed the heels of his hands into his eyes. He was saying, 'No, no, no,' over and over again and was bent almost double, like someone had actually punched him. I could see the soft skin at the back of his neck and I put my arms round him and held him, feeling his body shaking against me, trying to block the pictures flooding in my mind. I was crying now too, not caring about anything any more. I just held on for ages until he became still and he pulled away. His face was tight and his dark eyes were bloodshot and puffy.

'Luka, I'm so sorry,' I said.

He wiped his face with a shaky hand. 'I tried to go home,' he said. 'When I first . . . well, found myself in the fairground. But it was like something was pulling me back. I just couldn't do it. Maybe I didn't want to face it.'

He looked at me then with a desperate expression. 'Why am I here and not her?' he said. 'Why have I come back?'

'I don't know,' I said miserably. 'I just don't know.'

'I feel like she's here sometimes,' he said and he lifted his chin a little as though daring me to mock him. 'I can't see her, but I feel . . . something.'

We were silent for a moment. I didn't know what to say.

'Come and sit for a minute,' I said and, taking his hand, led him over to a low wall. I felt shy about touching him again, now the worst of the news was out, but held onto his hand anyway.

'It doesn't make any sense,' he said. 'She was a really good driver. She was always careful on that bend. There's no way she'd have driven too fast . . . unless . . .'

'Unless someone forced her off the road,' I finished the thought. 'But why?'

Luka reached into the pocket of his hoodie, which meant letting go of my hand.

'I don't know. But look, I found her camera,' he said, pulling out a battered leather case with a long strap.

'I went into the ghost train yesterday and found this wedged right near the back. It looks like someone tried to get it off her because the strap's broken.'

I gently took the leather case from Luka's fingers. He was right. I could see that the shoulder strap had been snapped, as though it had been pulled hard.

'Have you tried turning it on?' I said.

'Battery's dead,' said Luka. 'And someone has taken out the memory card.'

'Maybe she had some pictures someone wanted,' I said and Luka nodded.

'She used to say that a picture painted a thousand words. Her English was good, but she still sometimes couldn't find the right expressions and she got frustrated. It was like her photos were, I dunno, her voice sometimes.'

I could feel that he was getting himself together and I almost minded. I wanted to hold him again and had no excuse now. I felt ashamed and let out a big breath to try and clear my own head.

'So what now?' I said. 'We have nothing concrete, Luka. We don't know why someone was after her. We don't know anything, really.'

'No, but maybe that's why I'm here,' said Luka, his voice determined now. 'To find out what happened and get justice for Eva – and for me too, I guess. I don't know what I'm meant to do, but I know I can't do it alone, Bel. I wouldn't blame you for running a mile, though.'

He was looking into my eyes intently and, again, I saw his gaze move across my face in a way that made me hold my breath. I saw him swallow and he looked down. My stomach gave another little jump.

'I'm not going anywhere, Luka,' I whispered.

CHAPTER 17

Newcastle

I walked in the front door in a daze. Mum was on the phone and her face softened when she clocked me.

'Look, Bel's here now. Why don't you talk to her?' She handed me the phone and mumbled, 'It's your dad.'

Normally, I'd have grabbed it, but I hesitated, as though the phone were contaminated or something. The awful thing Mum said a few days before flashed into my mind.

'Bel? Is that my Jelly-B?'

'Hi, Dad.' My voice was flat.

'How are you, princess?'

'I'm okay, I guess. I miss you.'

'I miss you too, honey. Look, Bel, I've got some good news. Looks like I'm going to get there on Christmas Eve after all.'

'Oh. That's good.'

'Yeah, so we can have a proper Christmas.'

'Yeah.'

'And Bel . . .' He cleared his throat.

'Yeah?'

'We'll need to have some talks about stuff. Me, you and Mum.'

I didn't speak.

'Bel? You still there?'

'Yeah . . .'

'I'll explain everything properly in person, but I wanted to give you a heads up. I've been offered a job.'

'A job?' I said. 'That's good, right?'

'Well, thing is . . . it's in Newcastle.'

'But that's miles away! That's practically Scotland!'

I could hear Dad breathing heavily on the other end of the phone. I stared down at the small phone table that was covered in rubbish, including a business card from that Will bloke, which he'd obviously given Mum. I gave an inward tut.

'It's a really well-paid job, is the thing,' Dad was saying now. 'I'm not exactly in a position to turn it down. Look, I'll see you at Christmas and we'll talk properly then. Now put your mum back on.'

I handed her the phone without saying goodbye and went into the kitchen. I sat down at the table and listened to Mum speaking in that special high-pitched voice she reserved for Dad.

'I still don't understand why you can't just book a train

and let me know when you're getting in. We'll come and pick you up if you just tell me when.'

There was silence.

'But Steve . . .' She gave a huge sigh. 'Okay, look, I'm not really interested. I just wish for once you'd do things properly.'

I got up from the table and walked back into the hall then up the stairs. Even though I looked straight ahead, I could see Mum watching me as I left.

Once I was in my bedroom, I lay down on the bed, staring up at the ceiling. I could still hear the rumble of Mum's voice on the phone. I was glad I couldn't hear the actual words any more.

My thoughts were on a loop . . . The accident, Luka, Dad, Newcastle, the accident, Luka, Dad, Newcastle. A week ago I'd have asked Dad to take me with him. Newcastle had all sorts of good things. I was sketchy on the details but it wouldn't have been Slumpton, and me and Dad would have been together so nothing else would have mattered that much. But everything was different now. When I was in that old lady's house and I thought I'd lost Luka for ever . . . well, something had changed.

I knew I couldn't leave him now.

I had my face buried in my pillow when I heard the doorbell. Mum's bright visitor-voice floated up the stairs.

'Bel? Bel, come on down here,' said Mum. I decided to ignore her.

Minutes later there was a soft knock at my door.

I ignored that too but the knocking was insistent. I jumped up angrily and wrenched the bedroom door open.

'Oh!' I said. 'Sorry. I thought you were my mum.'

The girl from down the road was standing there, twiddling a strand of her long blond hair and blushing a little bit. 'Sorry,' she parroted. 'Your mum and then my mum insisted I came up here. My mum's organising one of her homeware crap parties. Look, I'll just make myself comfy here on the stairs and we can pretend we've had a huge bonding session if you like.'

My cheeks tweaked in an unfamiliar way. I realised I was smiling.

'No, that's okay,' I said. 'I'm Bel.'

She nodded. 'Yeah, I know. I'm Abbie.'

I waited for her to ask about my name, like most people did, but she said nothing, just looked at me as though trying to decide something.

'Um, do you want to come in?' I said and opened the door.

'Who wouldn't?' she said drily, and I blushed, suddenly seeing my bedroom through another's eyes. I hadn't bothered to put up any posters and my clothes were everywhere.

'I guess it is a bit of a mess,' I said.

'Yeah, but you have only just moved in,' she said kindly as she came inside. 'It's got potential.'

'It has?'

'Yeah, I love these skylights. Look, it's like my room. If you just do this . . .'

To my amazement, she kicked off her silver ballet flats and neatly stepped onto my unmade bed. She started battering the window frame. I'd never opened it before, what with it being DECEMBER and all, but after a lot of huffing and puffing and some bits of dried paint dusting her head, the window was open and letting in a sharp slice of air.

'Come see,' she said, her cheeks pink with exertion.

I cautiously climbed onto the bed, as though it was hers and not mine. I avoided her eyes, getting uncomfortably close to look out the window.

'Check that out,' she said and I gasped.

I could see the great grey slab of the sea in the distance and, because we were at the top of the hill, all the rooftops swished down in pretty patterns. There was smoke coming from a few chimneys and the sky was a swirl of bruised pink clouds.

'Wow!' It was all I could say.

'Yeah, Slumpton doesn't look so grim from a distance,' she said and I laughed.

'Abbiiiie!' an unfamiliar voice called from downstairs.

She rolled her eyes. 'Mein Kommandant's calling. Look, some people are coming round tomorrow evening. Friends from school. You're going to DS, right?'

It took me a minute to work out that she meant David Stafford. I nodded.

'Good. Why don't you come over too? About seven?'

A shy, happy feeling flushed my face. 'Yeah, I will. Thanks,' I said.

She bobbed her head in a casual goodbye and bounded down the stairs.

I climbed back on the bed again and poked my head out into the darkening sky. I still thought Slumpton was a dump but had to admit, it looked kind of pretty from up here. I breathed in the crisp air, thinking about Abbie's visit. It was nice to know there might be a friend for me here. One who was alive. It was all very well mooning about the place over Luka, but even if he liked me back, it was hard to imagine a future together. Could he ever be mine to keep?

CHAPTER 18

Window Bars

It was Saturday the next day and Mum wasn't working. I told myself that was the reason why I didn't rush straight out to the fairground again. It wasn't the whole story though.

Part of me was desperate to see Luka again and a couple of times I even started getting ready to go out. But something kept pulling me back. The fact that Luka was a ghost wasn't the problem, crazy as that sounds. It was the thought that he and Eva might have died because of something she knew.

Could they really have been *murdered*? It scared me, especially when I thought about the beating we'd witnessed in the fairground. This wasn't a world I recognised. If I walked away now, maybe I could be sure that I was safe. But was losing Luka a price I was prepared to pay?

The thoughts just kept see-sawing inside my head. I slumped around the house until Mum got in a strop and forced me to go with her into town.

We still hadn't spoken properly, not since the night of the slap. We walked down into the town centre in silence, Mum occasionally shooting glances my way.

'I tell you, I'm missing that old car!' she said finally, with a false laugh. We'd let Dad keep the car because he had to move around the country with the band.

I didn't respond.

'I must get on with buying Christmas stuff. Any ideas on what you'd like this year?' she said.

Oh, she was good.

'Still hoping for an iPod,' I said through my teeth.

'That might be a little bit beyond our budget this year, Bel,' said Mum. 'Is there anything else you fancy?'

'Yeah,' I said. 'My old life back.'

All you could hear after that was the clip-clop of Mum's boots as we walked along the icy pavement and the usual chorus of screeching seagulls that accompanied your every waking moment in this town.

Mum had to collect some dry cleaning from a shop on the outskirts of the town centre so we walked further than I'd gone before, in the opposite direction to the marina and fairground. When she came back out, her mobile rang. She seemed to get a lot of phone calls these days. I could tell instantly it was that Will bloke. She slightly turned her back to speak so I crossed over to a wall and leaned against it, not really wanting to hear her shamelessly flirting.

That's when I noticed the sign on the building next to me.

TMS Knitwear. Quality Fashions at Wholesale Prices.

For a second I stared blankly at it. And then it clicked. That was the name we'd seen on the flyer in Eva's ticket booth. It looked very unwelcoming. The windows had bars on them and there was a metal front door that would have withstood a tank.

Curious, I got up and walked around the side of the building. There was a small grubby window just out of reach. Looking quickly around, I climbed onto a loose pile of bricks from a sagging fence to get a peek inside.

I could see there were rows and rows of tables where women were working at sewing machines. Some of them had dark features and looked foreign and several of them weren't much older than me. A large man was standing at the end of the room, talking on a mobile phone, and when he turned, I almost fell down. It was the man with no neck I'd seen at the Town Hall and then beating up that man in the fairground. I drew back slightly but watched him turn to a girl who looked about sixteen. He shouted something right into her face. She cowered back in her chair like she was scared he would hit her.

Hot indignation blasted through me.

'Bel?'

I slipped and fell, gouging my knee on the brick.

Mum was staring at me.

'What on earth are you doing? Why are you looking in that window?'

I heard the back door being opened and I grabbed Mum's arm. 'Just being nosy,' I said hurriedly. 'Let's get home.' I pulled my protesting mother quickly away, too scared to look back and check if I'd been seen.

There was much harrumphing from Mum about my weird behaviour on the way home. But I tuned her out, trying to think.

Why had Eva kept that flyer? And did it have something to do with her and Luka's deaths?

My head was aching from it all.

I hoped going to Abbie's would help take my mind off things.

Back home, Mum was delighted when I told her I'd been invited round.

She moved my hair off my face with such a soft expression in her eyes that, for a moment, I thought I was going to crumple like a used tissue.

'Are you all right, Bel?'

I got up abruptly. 'I'm fine. Better get ready.'

I put on my favourite T-shirt, slicked on some lip-gloss and a wave of mascara. I didn't feel like dressing up, but Abbie looked quite stylish from what I'd seen and I wasn't going to have people from Slumpton looking down on me.

I looked at my slightly blurry reflection and took some

deep breaths. I felt nervous, like I'd forgotten how to be just a normal girl who thought ghosts were in stories and people only got beaten up on telly.

I had to get a grip.

It was after seven when I said goodbye to Mum and wound my woolly scarf around my neck. Mum insisted I took a torch with me because some of the streetlights were broken and she stood at the front door until I was out of sight. It was only me saying she would ruin my one and only friendship if she came with me that stopped her walking me all the way.

When I got to Abbie's, I looked up to the top window. I knew the skylight would be her bedroom because she'd said it was the same as mine. The window was open and strands of music and raucous laughter flew out like long streamers. There was a warm, orange glow and it looked so comforting. The safest, nicest place I could imagine.

But then I started thinking about the tender place at the back of Luka's neck for some reason and I suddenly wanted to see him so badly that my knees almost gave way. So what if there was something bad going on? Was I really going to let him deal with it alone?

I looked up at the welcoming window once again, heart thumping.

'Sorry, Abbie,' I whispered under my breath and started to run.

CHAPTER 19

A Perfect Fit

When I got to the fairground, I gasped at what I could see through the fence.

Some of the rides had been taken away and there were massive bald patches everywhere. The rollercoaster and the ghost train were still there, along with the stalls, but if it had felt desolate before, now it felt like it was pure sadness that howled through all the cracks in the hoardings.

He was gone. I just knew it. Maybe he thought I wasn't coming back and he'd moved on somewhere else. I stood there, not knowing what to do, feeling like I wanted to cry. I had to make myself go in there to be sure. Even with a torch and the moonlight illuminating everything brightly, the thought of being in there alone was awful. I took a deep breath. I was going to look for

Luka if it killed me. With trembling hands, I fed one of the tickets into the turnstile.

Once inside, I looked around and shivered.

The edges of everything stood out sharply in the crisp air and there were long shadows cast by the remaining bits of equipment. The sky was covered with great smears of stars I'd never been able to see in London. I swallowed deeply and I forced myself to walk further into the fairground.

'Luka?' I called out tentatively. It felt wrong to speak any louder. There was no reply, just the distant crash and whoosh of the sea.

I walked around for a bit, but he wasn't anywhere obvious. I didn't know what to do now. I looked at my watch. It was too late to go to Abbie's, but it was too early to go home. I'd agreed ten with Mum and it was only eight.

My heart was in my boots. I didn't want to go home and I didn't want to hang around here, alone. I was just about to walk towards the exit when I found myself going the other way. I had the weirdest urge to look at Eva's photos again. I don't know why. Maybe it was because they were so full of life and colour and everything else here felt so dead. Or maybe it was just because they were connected to Luka.

The door of the ticket booth was still open and I went inside, carefully checking for giant cobwebs. I scanned the wall. The cute picture of little Luka made me smile. Then I spotted another one of him next to it that I hadn't noticed the other day.

It looked recent. His hair was being blown by the wind and he was making a face as though protesting at the picture, but smiling, eyes shining. I touched his face with my finger. When it was taken, he was alive. Just a normal good-looking boy who probably had loads of girlfriends. If I'd met him then, would he even have looked at me twice?

Guiltily, I pulled the picture down and stuffed it into my pocket.

I looked around again and realised something. There was one place I hadn't checked for Luka.

The ghost train.

I bit my lip, paralysed with indecision. I couldn't bear the thought of going into that creepy ride alone, at night.

I forced myself to think it through. Tomorrow was Christmas Eve and Mum wouldn't be back at work for ages. It was going to be really difficult to get over here during the holidays. And I still didn't know where he would go when the fairground got demolished in the New Year. The thought that I might never see Luka again made me close my eyes for a moment. When I opened them, I tried to breathe slowly. I had to check out the ghost train.

I came out of the booth and looked back into the fairground, still hesitating. An owl hooted somewhere nearby. My nervous breaths were making hazy clouds in the cold air.

Stop being such a baby, Bel. It's only a cheesy ride.

I forced myself back into the fairground, trying to convince myself it was no big deal, but all my courage had dribbled away anyway by the time I got to the entrance of the ghost train. I stood there, vibrating all over with terror and cold and then forced myself to peek tentatively inside. Just off to the left, I could see a row of switches and remembered Luka fiddling with them the day I had my ride. I batted the memory of the spooky whispering away like a fly, even though it made adrenalin flood through me. If I could just get the lights on, it would be okay. I stepped cautiously into the entrance and took small steps forward, my torch sending a pathetic blob of white light in front of me.

There was a bunch of rags in the corner. Just before I reached the switches, the bunch of rags started to rustle and move, before slowly rising up.

'ARGHHHHHHH!' I went and 'ARGHHHHHHH' went the rags as I dropped the torch and tore back the way I'd come.

Luka appeared outside about two seconds later, his hair sticking up like a brush and his eyes wide.

'What were you doing in there, Luka?!' I yelled.

'I was sleeping!' he yelled back. 'What were YOU doing?'

We stared at each other, panting slightly from shock, and then in the same split second we both started howling with hysterical laughter.

Luka had the funniest laugh ever, like 'Her-her-her-her!' He was wiping his eyes and clutching his stomach.

After a bit, we calmed down and just grinned at each other, goofily.

'I couldn't find you,' I said, 'I thought you'd . . .'

'I didn't think you'd come back . . .'

We both spoke at once then grinned again.

'You first,' said Luka.

'Why were you sleeping in that creepy old place?' I asked.

'You may have noticed they're taking my luxury pad apart,' he said.

I nodded to where the creepy policeman doll used to be. 'Yeah. They've even taken laughing boy away.'

'Yeah,' sighed Luka, following my gaze. 'I quite miss that crazy guy.' He looked at me again. 'I just wanted somewhere to shelter. It gets a bit lonely and spooky in here at night.'

'Surely you're not frightened of ghosts?' I said with a smile, but he didn't smile back and I wished I hadn't said it.

Luka cleared his throat in a stagey way and then turned to look at me. His dark eyes looked tired and I fought the overwhelming urge to stroke his cheek.

'Um, Bel . . .' he started to say. 'I . . .' but I clutched his arm because I realised I could hear something floating up through the floor. It was that whispering noise again, coming from inside the ghost train, but louder now. We stared at each other, wide-eyed.

'There it is again,' I hissed. 'I told you there was something.'

We stood there like statues, trying to make out what was being said but it was just beyond our reach. I had the strangest feeling that if I could just make out the words, I wouldn't be scared.

'I hear that at night sometimes,' said Luka quietly.

I looked at him.

'I sometimes think it's Eva,' he said. 'You know, trying to send me a message or something.' He sighed. 'But it's not working if she is. And why here of all places?'

'I don't know.' I shivered. 'Come on, let's go.'

Luka walked me back towards the entrance.

'Doesn't seem like we've got much further, does it?' I said.

'I guess not,' he said.

We stopped near the gates.

'Er, Luka . . .' I began. 'It's Christmas Eve tomorrow and my mum's off work. I'm not sure if I'll be able to get back here for a few days.'

'Oh,' he said in a flat voice. 'Right.'

'I can't help it being Christmas!'

He gave a tight smile. 'I know. It's just . . . well, it sort of . . . keeps me going, seeing you.'

I was so taken aback by this, my next words tumbled out too fast. 'I'll come back as soon as I can, I promise. I want to see you too.' All my defences were melting by the second and tears blurred my vision.

'Aw, come on. Don't go making that piggy face again, Ann-aaa-belle,' said Luka and I laughed a bit hysterically.

'I warned you about calling me that!' I hiccupped

and went to play hit him but he caught my hand and held onto it. We both straightened our arms and our fingers linked together easily. I went to wipe my tears with my other hand but Luka's was suddenly there instead. I felt the gentle pressure of his fingers across my cheek and shivered.

And then his face was very close. I saw his long lashes like two black semicircles as he closed his eyes and his cool lips touched mine.

It wasn't the first time I'd kissed a boy. It wasn't even the second. But the other times had been wet and pushy with not much pleasure involved. This . . . this was very different. Our mouths were a perfect fit. I swear it was like the dark, desolate fairground melted away and I could almost hear laughter and music from the rides and sense bright, colourful lights swirling around us. Just for a moment, amid all the bad stuff, this was a happy place again.

When we finally broke apart, he held me close and I squeezed back, hard, trying to breathe him in and wishing I could stop time and live in this moment for ever.

'Merry Christmas, Bel,' he whispered.

'Merry Christmas, Luka.'

CHAPTER 20

Comfort and Joy

'And this is just a little something extra from me, Jelly-B.'

Dad reached behind the cushion on the sofa and handed me a small, wrapped package. Mum looked at him sharply but his eyes were only on me, twinkling.

He'd turned up late on Christmas Eve. I'd tried to stay awake, but by eleven-thirty I couldn't keep my eyes open any longer. Voices from downstairs had lured me back to consciousness.

'I can't believe you actually went to the pub before coming here!' Mum's voice went rat-at-at-at, like a gun. Dad's, though, was mellow as hot chocolate.

'I've been travelling since this morning,' he said, 'and I needed a bit of Dutch courage, if you must know. I only went in for one.'

'Well, your daughter tried to stay awake but she's only a child. You'll have to see her in the morning.'

'Dad!'

I shot down the stairs and into his arms at full-pelt. His battered old leather jacket smelled of cigarettes and Daddishness. He hugged me for ages, his chin resting on the top of my head.

Then he held me back and looked at me, both of us grinning like crazy.

His hair had got longer and I could see grey in his stubbly chin. He looked the same but different all at once. There was a beery smell on his breath and his eyes were a bit red.

'Sorry, I'm so late,' he said. 'I didn't mean to wake you up. You look about five years older. This sea air is obviously good for you!'

I wanted to reply but to my horror I wasn't able to speak at all. I clung onto him, hiding my face in his jacket.

Dad just hugged me harder, making little shushing noises and saying, 'Hey, now, what's all this?'

I wanted to tell him everything . . . about how horrible it was here, about Luka, about how scared I was about starting school. But I couldn't speak.

He hugged me a bit longer and then Mum packed me off to bed.

I woke the next morning feeling excited about Christmas for the first time.

I could see that Dad had slept on the sofa. He was outside having a cigarette when I came down and he turned and waved through the kitchen window. His face was all creased and Mum's eyes looked swollen, but we had Christmassy music on and even the stupid old fake tree didn't look too bad as I got amongst my presents.

Mum had bought small things for Dad – just some socks and the smelly shower stuff he liked. But when she unwrapped the present from him – an expensive-looking velvet scarf with little beads sewn into it – she'd stared down at it in her lap for a moment, stroking it like a cat. Then she'd thanked him stiffly, avoiding his eyes.

That was when he said the thing about having something extra for me.

I unwrapped the paper carefully and inside was a see-through plastic box containing a shiny blue, impossibly beautiful, brand new iPod.

'Dad!' I flung my arms round his neck.

'Now then,' he chuckled. 'Just make sure you don't put any rubbish on it, because I'll be checking.'

Mum got up sharply from her seat and left the room. I saw Dad watch her go and then heard some banging around in the kitchen. Dad gave a heavy sigh and got up, winking at me before following her out of the room.

They were talking quietly at first, with the kitchen door shut. I tried to turn up the telly and ignore them, eating my selection box and stroking my iPod. Mum was probably just jealous, but my stomach went all cold and sore, like it always did when they fought, and the chocolate tasted like wood. Soon they were shouting.

Snatches drifted into the room like a bad smell. I could mainly hear Mum.

'You haven't paid a penny since we moved and then you go flinging money on expensive presents you can't afford? And when are you going to tell her, Steve? I'm fed up with being the bad guy.'

I forced myself to my feet and walked to the kitchen as though about to be strapped into the electric chair. I didn't want to do it but I knew I had to.

I pushed open the door and Mum and Dad instantly stopped arguing and stared at me like a couple of gormless fish.

'Tell me what?' I said and Dad shot a furious look at Mum.

'Now look what you've done,' he hissed, but Mum just tipped her chin, defiantly.

'Your child has a right to know what's going on,' she said, her voice trembling.

I felt my knees buckle so hard I had to sit down. Dad came over and swung another chair round the other way in one easy movement. His face was a picture of concern and guilt as he sat down.

'Bel,' he said. 'The thing is, me and your mum aren't really together any more and haven't been for a long time.'

'Just tell her,' said Mum in a flat voice.

'I'm getting to it!' he snapped and Mum turned away and stood at the sink, looking out.

'And while I've been away, I've become . . . close to someone else.'

I jumped up from the table so my chair screeched. 'No, no, I don't even want to hear this,' I said, covering my ears. I went to leave the room but Dad grabbed my arm.

'Sweetheart, it doesn't mean I don't want you any more. But things change. People change. Sometimes relationships have to move on.'

I shook my arm free and stormed out.

'It only happened when we'd already split up!' he called after me but I ran up the stairs, still covering my ears.

Just after, I heard the front door slam so hard the house shook.

Needless to say, it was the worst Christmas Day in the history of time.

Dad came back eventually, looking very sheepish, but I made it clear I didn't want to talk about any of it any more. We ate turkey and watched telly in virtual silence. Dad wanted to load the software for my new iPod but when he realised we had no internet connection he lost his temper, kicking the table when he thought I wasn't looking.

The only thing that made any of it bearable was thinking about Luka and replaying our goodbye kiss over and over in my mind. It was like being in prison and I even thought about sneaking out to see him but knew I'd never get away with it. So I just endured the long, long day and, when bedtime came, I was grateful. The atmosphere was horrible in the house and it was only when I was in my bedroom that I felt I could breathe properly.

* * *

In the morning, I turned over in bed and an emptiness in the air told me Dad had gone.

I ran downstairs and found Mum sitting at the kitchen table in her dressing gown, cradling a hot mug of coffee. Her eyes were red and her hair was all over the place.

'Where's Dad?' I said, and my voice sounded too big for the room. She pushed a piece of paper across the table with a weak smile.

'He had to get off early. He left this for you.' She paused. 'Look, honey . . .'

I ignored her and snatched the envelope, which had *Bel* on the front in his loopy handwriting. He hardly ever called me that, usually preferring silly nicknames. I swallowed and opened the envelope.

Bel
I'm sorry I didn't see you this morning but there is only one train out of town with it being Boxing Day. I'm so sorry too about what I had to tell you yesterday and about me and Mum fighting. I want you to know that what's going on between us has nothing to do with you and that we both love you very much. I'm going to try to get down to see you again sometime in January and once I get established in Newcastle, I'm planning to show you all the sights and give you some brilliant visits. You'll like Sarah once you meet her, really you will.

Keep strong, JB, and remember your old dad isn't perfect but he loves you always.

Dad XXXX

I went back to bed without a word and lay there, staring at the ceiling. I knew now that we were never going to be a proper family again.

CHAPTER 21

Out With the Old

By about one p.m. I was thoroughly sick of myself. I had a shower and got dressed. When I went downstairs, Mum was in exactly the same position but now there was a half-empty glass of wine in front of her and she was sitting in a cloud of blue smoke. She made a pathetic attempt to bat away the very obvious evidence of her recent cigarette when I walked into the room.

I rolled my eyes. At least she had the decency to blush.

I made myself some toast and Marmite. I couldn't face any rows so I was careful to clean the knife in between spreads. I sat down at the table. Mum now had her face in her hands, which were threaded through her hair in a way that stretched her face in a weird way.

She let out a huge sigh and sat back in her seat,

looking around the kitchen. 'God, this place is a dump,' she said suddenly.

I almost choked on my toast. Was this really Mrs Oh-You'll-Soon-Love-It-Here speaking? I just gawped at her, my toast held in mid-air.

'What?' she said. 'Don't you think *I* was sad about leaving London too? Don't you think I miss *my* friends? Or wish I could have just sold this place and booked a nice holiday for us with the money instead?'

'I dunno, I —'

She cut across me. 'Because I was and I do. I loved it here when I used to visit my great aunt as a little girl, but I never wanted to live here. Whether we like it or not though, it's the way it is. So we might as well get used to it. And I tell you what I'm going to do right now . . .'

It must have been the wine. Mum was never like this. To my astonishment, she pulled her chair over to the sink, clambered on and then ripped off a great big strip of the nasty green wallpaper.

I had my hands over my mouth, giggles bubbling up inside like gas.

Mum turned round, grinning at me. 'Well, that feels good,' she said. 'Don't just sit there like a lemon. Why don't you start over there?'

For the next three hours, we ripped and tugged and pulled down every bit of horrible wallpaper we could find. Mum put the radio on and we sang along to pop songs while we worked, and by the time Mum filled the last bin bag in the house, we were both covered in bits of old plaster and aching in every conceivable bit of our bodies.

We looked at each other and started to laugh. Mum put out her arms and, because it seemed like the easiest thing in the world, I walked into them and put my arms round her. I'd grown since we'd last hugged and we were almost the same height now. I heard a big sniff and squeezed my eyes shut. I didn't want to cry again. I'd cried so much in the last twenty-four hours that I felt like I had no spare liquid left in my body. Mum let go eventually and wiped her eyes.

'Right,' she said briskly, 'you put those bin bags out the front and I'll put together some turkey and leftovers from yesterday. We'll get cleaned up and see what's on telly.'

I opened the front door, humming a little, and then jumped as I realised someone was coming along the pavement.

It was Abbie, in a sparkly top and soft cardigan that were obviously brand new. She also wore a grim expression.

'My mum wants you and your mum to come over for a drink,' she said flatly. 'And you've got something in your hair.'

I pulled the dangling piece of wallpaper away with an embarrassed laugh and then met her eyes, which were like stones. I'd obviously really hurt her feelings by not showing up before.

'Look, Abbie, about the other night,' I began . . .

'Mum says to come at seven-thirty,' she said and turned crisply away.

I hated knowing I'd hurt her feelings and I had no idea how to make it up to her.

When I passed on the invitation, Mum was enthusiastic.

It was only when we were putting on our coats that something hit me.

Mum thought I'd been at Abbie's the other night, when really I'd been kissing Luka.

Would she say something? Abbie owed me nothing. I had no way of knowing if I could trust her. I just had to hope she wasn't going to drop me in it.

CHAPTER 22

They're Everywhere You Look

Abbie's house was a riot of Christmas music and tinsel. Her mum opened the door with a huge glass of red wine in one hand and a sausage roll in the other. She greeted us like we were long-lost friends.

'Come in, come in!' she said as one of her bra straps broke free from the black dress she was wearing and escaped down her bare shoulder. She had the same eyes and face shape as Abbie, but her hair was darker, pulled back messily into a scrunchie.

'It's nice to meet you both,' she said and Mum smiled in a puzzled way. She opened her mouth to point out that I had met her before and then Abbie, miraculously, appeared at the top of the stairs.

'Come on up,' she said and, despite the lack of enthusiasm in her voice, I grabbed the invitation like a life raft.

Abbie's room was like mine with an extreme makeover. Her walls were painted a deep mustard yellow. Lamps cast a warm glow in the corners and she'd hung gauzy scarves from the picture rails behind her bed so it looked a bit like a four-poster. The bed itself was loaded with sparkly, tasselled cushions. I half expected a buff man in a pair of Aladdin trousers to appear and offer me a tray of Turkish Delight.

'Wow,' was all I could say.

She regarded me in that cool way she had and slumped back on the bed. She didn't suggest I sit down too, so I stood there awkwardly for a minute before perching on the end.

'Great room.'

Silence.

She wasn't going to help me out here, clearly. There was only one thing I could think to do. I reached into my pocket and found the now slightly rumpled picture of Luka.

I held it up and I could see she was interested because her nose practically twitched, like a fox. She leaned a bit closer, despite herself. 'Who's that?' she said finally.

'He's the reason I didn't turn up before,' I said, 'and my mum will kill me if you let on. So right now I'm throwing myself at your mercy.'

I could see humour in her eyes, although her mouth wasn't ready to play yet.

'Good luck with that,' she said.

Smiles crept up both our faces.

'Give it here then,' she said, reaching for the photo. She studied it for ages. 'Cute boy,' she said.

I felt a rush of pride. 'Yeah.' I suddenly wanted to tell her everything, but she would only think I was insane.

From downstairs the sounds of Slade and raucous laughter drifted upwards like smoke.

'But here's the thing,' I said. 'He's not here for much longer. He's going away to . . . Newcastle.' The name popped out before I'd known I was going to say it. It just seemed easier to say he was going away than explain any of the real situation.

'Can't you stay in touch? You can always IM him,' said Abbie and I mentally kicked myself for bringing moving up in the first place.

'His mum and dad are, er, a bit strict so he isn't allowed a computer,' I said finally.

'That's sucky,' she said in a kinder voice and I met her eyes, grateful.

'Yeah, it really is. Look, I'm sorry I didn't come the other evening.'

'It's no big deal, really,' she said.

I curled my legs up under me and got comfy on the cushions. 'Come on then,' I said, feeling myself relax. 'Give me the lowdown on The Place With The Lurid Purple Uniform . . .'

So she did. She told me about avoiding certain toilets because of the 'witches' from Year Eleven who hung out there, and about the psycho PE teacher who took netball. She also told me about the great drama group she was in after school. She told me about growing up in Slumpton and how she couldn't wait to leave, but also about the beach parties she and her friends had last summer, when they made bonfires. Once, the sound of the sea lulled them to sleep so they all missed their curfews.

For the next hour or so we chatted and I did a pretty good impersonation of being a normal girl, and then her mum called us downstairs for food. We reluctantly got up from the bed.

Laughing and chatting, we went into the noisy living room that seemed to have drunken adults sitting in every corner. I spotted Mrs Longmeadow taking up most of a sofa and then noticed Mum sitting on another in close conversation with Will. She caught my eye when I came in and didn't even look embarrassed.

Me and Abbie got some food and carried on chatting, draped over the big floor cushions. I tried to avoid looking at Mum. What I'd been told about Dad, and now her and Will . . . well, it just wasn't something I wanted to think about.

It was when I was helping myself to seconds of Abbie's mum's delicious trifle that I caught a snatch of conversation from Mrs L.

'I just don't know why there has to be so many of

them,' she was saying. 'They're everywhere you look. I even saw two girls no older than your Abigail begging outside Morrison's the other day. Looked like gypsies. I think they should send the lot of them back where they belong.'

A couple of the other adults were nodding and murmuring agreement. Mum was staring at her drink. I know that anywhere else she would have piled in and challenged Mrs Longmeadow. I saw Will making a face and getting to his feet.

'We've spoken about this before. I think it's about time I got you home, Mum,' he said, but Mrs L wasn't for budging.

She looked at him, frowning. 'What, don't you think most people round here feel that way?' she said.

'I don't feel that way,' said Will in a stern, quiet voice and there were a couple of 'No, me neither's' including one from Mum, but most people didn't say anything at all. Abbie's mum, obviously flustered by the change in atmosphere in the room, jumped up.

'Come on, everyone,' she said in a jolly voice. 'Must be time to top up drinkies.'

Later in bed, I thought about what Luka had said before. If something bad happened to his mum, how many people felt like Mrs Longmeadow about foreigners and turned a blind eye? I pictured the clothing factory and the way that girl was so frightened of the man who looked like her boss.

I'd seen him with that businessman Lex McAllistair

outside the marina. Eva had worked in the fairground, which was being pulled down *because* of the marina. Eva knew something that someone had wanted kept quiet. I rolled over, wide awake now. It felt like there was some connection there, if only I could see it. Somehow, the marina seemed at the centre of it all.

If I could just find out something really useful . . . well, maybe Luka would understand that he'd been right to ask for my help. Maybe he would know that he wasn't really alone.

I decided I was going to have to find a way to get inside the marina and have a look about.

Mum was a bit fragile the next morning and was still in bed at ten when I got up.

I took her some juice in bed to butter her up and then casually dropped in that I was going out as I was leaving the room.

'Wait up. I'll have a quick shower and come with you,' she said. 'It'll clear my head. I knew I shouldn't have drunk all that wine.' She winced.

Panic flared inside me. 'No!' I said. 'I mean, if it's OK, I'd like to have some time alone. You know, to think about everything. About you and Dad splitting up.' I felt a bit guilty but I reckoned, if I was going to be the child of a broken home, I'd earned the right to use it to my advantage.

Mum sank back into her pillows. 'Of course, love. I understand. Just, you know, wrap up warmly.'

I got to the door and she spoke again. 'Bel?'

I turned round.

'It'll all be okay, you'll see.'

It had rained heavily the night before and everything felt like it had been freshly washed. As I got near the seafront, an image flashed into my mind of Abbie's beach parties. They did sound kind of fun. For a moment, I pictured me and Luka huddled together with a blanket round our shoulders, sharing a bag of hot chips and laughing and kissing, the waves lapping the shore and our skin smelling of salt and sunshine. We'd be like normal people. With a future.

A great wave of sadness punched me somewhere near the kidneys. We would never be a normal couple. How could we?

The closer I got to the marina, the more I talked myself out of this stupid plan.

It was madness. I had no way of getting in and I didn't even know what I was looking for. I decided to just go and have a look from the outside, just in case I came up with a bright idea.

When I got there, I noticed two things.

One, the gates were open wide because a lorry was at the entrance ready to deliver something.

And two, the security guard was having a conversation with the lorry driver and not paying attention.

Before my brain could talk them out of it, my legs had taken me inside the gates.

CHAPTER 23

Teeth and Skin

It felt like an ant colony inside. There were huge cranes and diggers everywhere and tons of men scurrying around and looking busy. There was a long row of buildings that looked half finished and then another section covered with cranes that led out towards the water.

I felt like an ant with no job. Slacker ant. What was worse, I was trespassing and could get into a whole lot of trouble for even being here. The air was filled with dust and the sound of those screeching saws that make your ears hurt.

I could see two men in yellow hard hats with clipboards walking towards me and talking in an animated way. There was nowhere to hide except a portakabin next to me, which had a door slightly ajar.

Because I couldn't think of anything else to do, I leapt up the step and went inside.

It was an office, judging by the desks and filing cabinets and had an air of someone having just popped out. There was even a cup of steaming coffee on the desk and a half-smoked cigarette in a cracked saucer. Just behind the desk was a small safe, which had been left open slightly. I looked around quickly and then peeked inside, expecting to see money or important papers.

Instead, it was stuffed with small booklets in bundles, with different coloured hard covers. I grabbed one and ripped the elastic band off, my hands shaking.

It looked like a passport, written in an alphabet I didn't understand. The photo showed a man in his twenties with black hair and a thin, dark moustache. Flicking through the books, I found that they were all passports. Some of the people in the photos had dark complexions and some had high cheekbones and some looked Chinese. Lots of the photos were of young women and I gasped as I recognised the girl I'd seen in the factory. Her name was Lili Babic.

I heard voices right outside the portakabin then and I looked around in a panic. There was a pile of old dust sheets covered in streaks of paint in the corner on a chair and I threw myself across the room and underneath them just as the door opened and the cabin vibrated with heavy footsteps.

It was really stuffy and the sheets reeked of paint and made me dizzy but I tried to stay as still as I could, even though I was sure my heart was beating so loud that anyone could hear it. I tried to breathe quietly and slowly, listening hard. I could hear two men talking and I realised I'd heard one of the voices before. But where? Then it hit me. I'd heard it on the telly. It was Lex McAllistair.

'I'm not really interested in the excuses. We just need more manpower,' he said. 'We've made up a lot of time but we're still behind by a long way.'

'I know,' said the other man, 'but we've had problems with customs contacts at Dover and Folkestone and it's getting harder to get them in.'

There was a pause before McAllistair spoke again.

'What about that whinger who had the accident? Did you deal with him?'

There was a pause. 'Well, that's something, I guess,' he said. 'Hey! Did you leave this open? What were you thinking?'

There was an angry discussion about this and just when I thought I was going to suffocate, I heard the voices recede and the door of the portakabin was closed. I counted to fifty and then tentatively peeked out of the pile of sheets.

Thank God they'd gone. I carefully opened the door and came down the steps, looking around. I just needed to get to the exit.

'Oi! What the hell were you doing in there?' The man's voice, suddenly right there, jolted through me like an electric shock.

'I'm just, I . . .' My mouth flapped open and closed like

a fish as I started to back away. It was Lex McAllistair.

'You're not allowed in here,' he barked. 'What do you think you're doing?'

My brain was forming words like, 'Really sorry, didn't mean to, better be going,' but I was so scared I couldn't speak.

His mouth opened a little bit as something occurred to him. He grabbed my arm with a meaty hand.

'Hey, were you mooching about in my office just now? What were you doing in there? What do you want?'

I just did the only thing I could think of, and sank my teeth into his hand like a dog. He gave a roar of pain and tried to grab me again, but I ran at full-pelt back towards the entrance where, thank God, the gates were still open. I hurled myself through them and sprinted for my life.

When I felt it was safe to stop and look behind me, I could see that no one was following. I bent and rested my hands on my knees, shaking violently all over and trying to catch my breath. My stomach ached and I felt like I might throw up but also had a crazy urge to laugh hysterically.

I knew I had to see Luka and tell him, even though I'd already been out for ages and was probably going to have Mum on my back about it later. I didn't really understand what was going on in that marina, but I was now sure it had something to do with what happened to him and Eva.

As I got closer to the fairground, I walked faster, desperate to see him now.

It was easy to find him this time because he was

sitting on the lowest bit of the rollercoaster, his legs dangling over the side. I looked up at him. I hadn't seen him since the kiss and half of me felt shy, but half of me wanted to just grab him and do it again.

But I could tell something was wrong straight away. Luka's face was blank and unwelcoming.

'Don't make me come up there,' I said, shaking my fist and his sombre face twitched a bit but he didn't smile. He jumped down so he was standing in front of me. He still didn't speak and something anxious twisted inside me. 'What's wrong? Are you all right?'

He flicked a harsh look at me. 'I'm blinding, Bel,' he said in a stony voice. 'I've never been better in my life. I'm dead and I spend my days alone in a fairground. Who wouldn't love that?'

Stung, I just stared at him, not knowing what to say. But he hadn't finished.

'Did you have a lovely Christmas then?' he said. 'Lots of nice presents with Mumsie and Daddy? Did you enjoy your turkey with all the trimmings?'

So that's what his problem was. 'I did warn you that I couldn't come for a couple of days, Luka. I wanted to, but I —'

'Did you?' he interrupted.

I stared at him, confused.

'Did you really want to see me?' he said. It was like he was spitting out sour pips every time he spoke.

'Of course I did! What is it, Luka? Why are you being like this?'

He kicked at a loose stone with his toe and stared at the ground. There was a pause before he spoke again.

'I dunno, Bel, I just think you've been sitting around pulling crackers and having fun and I've been sitting here, completely alone in this old dump, that's all.'

I felt a flash of bright anger. 'Just for your information,' I said, 'it was the worst Christmas of my life actually, Luka. My parents are splitting up and they had a massive row on Christmas Day.' My breath was coming fast now and I couldn't seem to stop. 'So you're not the only person with problems.'

He had a mean smile on his face when he spoke again. 'Yeah, but I don't really think there's a comparison between you and me, is there? You've got everything in front of you still. You've got a future. What do I have? Nothing. I don't even know how I got here.'

I knew if I could tell him what had happened earlier, it might help break this weird mood he was in.

'Look, Luka I —'

But he wasn't going to let me speak. 'So I don't really know why you even bothered to come back, to tell you the truth,' he went on. 'I'll probably move on soon and you'll forget all about me. You can get on with your nice little life and it'll be like I was never here. You can hang around with boys who still have a heartbeat.' He was breathing heavily now, like he'd been running. 'What's wrong with you anyway? Why would you want to be with a freak like me?'

Tears started to prickle my eyes. 'Luka, don't . . .' I

whispered, but whatever had been going through his mind these last two days was working like poison.

He dusted down his jeans in a decisive way. 'Look at it this way, Bel. I'm doing you a favour. No questions asked, no one hurt. I'm letting you go.' There was a wobble in his voice now.

'What if I don't want to go?' I said, squeezing my hands into fists by my sides.

'*I* want you to go,' he said quietly.

I felt like I'd been slapped across the face. I turned away, blinking back hot tears. I thought I heard him say, 'Wait,' quietly, but I didn't turn around and I just walked away.

He'd made his feelings for me pretty clear.

CHAPTER 24

Bluebird

I stumbled away, so upset that, when I walked past the marina, I didn't notice the car following me at first.

It was only when I was almost home that I realised a black 4x4 with darkened windows and a number plate that read *MCA 2* was driving very slowly behind me. I stopped and the car stopped. I started walking and the car moved away again. It carried on all the way to my front door and, when I put my key in the lock with fumbling fingers, it sped away from the kerb leaving a cloud of exhaust. I knew in that split second that it was one of McAllistair's men behind the wheel, especially with that number plate. They didn't know who I was or why I'd been looking in that safe but they wanted to scare me. It must have been pretty obvious I'd been snooping in there. If those passports were somehow connected to what happened to Luka and Eva, they'd want to make sure I didn't come back.

Following me home was a clear message to keep my nose out. I started to shiver so hard with fright, my teeth chattered as I burst through the front door.

I was a nervous wreck all evening and kept looking outside the window to see if the car came back. When a black van pulled up outside I almost peed myself, until I realised it was just a delivery for the people next door.

Mum kept asking me if I was all right and stealing glances at me, but I just told her I had a headache. I went to bed early and curled up on my duvet, trying not to remember the look on Luka's face and his hard words. Part of me thought he hadn't really wanted me to go. But he'd told me to leave, hadn't he?

My thoughts went round and round my head until I finally fell into a feverish, whispery sleep filled with bad dreams. I dreamt that water was covering my head and I was banging on glass, trying to get free. Then I dreamt that I was following Luka and trying to catch him, but every time I got close, he would melt further away. I woke up feeling way more tired than when I'd gone to bed and lay there for ages with everything churning round inside.

It was the dripping tap that got me out of bed eventually. All I could hear was its slow drumming in the bathroom until I thought I'd go mad. So much for Will sorting it out. I knew and he knew and Mum knew that the whole DIY thing was just a ruse anyway.

That made me think about Dad and his new woman. I started imagining them getting married and maybe even having a baby together. Why not? He could have a whole new family in Newcastle. I wouldn't be his special girl any more.

Then I started thinking about Luka again and how he'd told me to go and the cloud hanging over me got about a hundred times heavier.

I walked over to my desk and picked up his photo. Tracing the line of his jaw with my finger, I remembered how his dark lashes had looked when he'd closed his eyes to kiss me. My stomach swooped as I relived the moment our lips had touched.

Then I put the photo face down on my desk.

I was about to walk away when I noticed the papers we'd found in the booth were also still on my desk. I picked one of them up curiously. The world seemed to have changed so much in only a week and so much had happened. I flipped over the flyer.

Contact Bluebird?

Why had Eva written that? What did it mean?

Luka had told me to go away but I couldn't let it go now. I was involved in this whether he liked it or not. I decided to at least try and do a bit of research online and then swore when I remembered we still didn't have our broadband working.

I was thinking about whether Slumpton had such a thing as an internet café when I heard Mum's key in the door. She was on a half day today. But she wasn't alone. I could hear that Will was with her.

I quickly got dressed. When I went downstairs, Will and Mum were at the table drinking tea and Dylan was zooming around the floor playing with a huge toy Batmobile that was making a whole series of deeply annoying noises.

Will smiled at me, a bit warily. I didn't smile back.

'Mum, when are we going to get the computer connected? I want to get my iPod working and see if I've got any emails.'

I got a guilty pang when I thought about my recent text silence with Jasmine. It felt like there was too much to say now. How could I have a normal conversation when all this was going on around me? It felt like my brain just had too much stuffed into it to handle worrying about that right now. I didn't need any more reasons to feel bad.

Mum sighed. 'I'm sorry, Bel, I just haven't time to get anyone out.' She smiled at Will. 'It's just one of the hundred and four things that I've been meaning to do since we moved in.'

Will turned to me. 'I can't help with iTunes, but if you just want to look at your emails, you could go next door and use the PC I bought for Mum. I thought she might quite fancy being a silver surfer, but she hasn't looked at the thing since I got her hooked up,' he said in his plummy voice.

Mum laughed as though he'd said something hilariously funny.

'Is she in?' I asked suspiciously and I saw a knowing look pass across his face.

'No, she's out visiting her sister, so you'd have the house all to yourself.'

Result. I almost smiled at him. 'All right, then. Thanks.'

Mum cocked an eyebrow at me as Will got up to let me in next door.

Mrs Longmeadow's house was exactly like ours, except every possible surface was covered in flowered material, which made your eyes go a bit funny until you got used to it. It also smelled strongly of Mrs Longmeadow's perfume.

There was lots of Dylan's stuff all over the place in the spare room upstairs and a pair of small pyjama bottoms were lying on the floor. There was a bed in there, plus a small computer table, chair and PC. It was a much nicer computer than ours and I thought what a waste it was, sitting up here gathering dust. Imagine all the revolting illnesses Mrs L could investigate with it. Will crawled about on the floor plugging things in, his big body filling the small space. I realised I had no idea where Dylan's mum was and decided to ask Mum about it later. Maybe he'd accidentally smothered her in one of his horrible rugby shirts.

'There you go,' he said after a moment. 'All yours. Take as long as you like.'

Yeah, and that'll give you plenty of time to chat up my mum, I thought.

'Thanks, but I won't need long,' I said instead.

'Okay, just close it down when you're done,' he said.

'Oh and, er, Will . . .' It felt strange and wrong to use his name.

'Yes, Bel?'

'What do Folkestone, Dover and Harwich have in common?'

He gave me a curious look. 'They're all international ports . . . Why?'

'Just wondered,' I said and turned to the computer.

Now I was here, and Will was gone, I wasn't sure where to start. I tentatively checked my emails first and got a happy surge in my chest when I saw there were about four from Jasmine and a couple from other friends. Jas's started off all chatty but the last one didn't have a message but just said *Where R U?* in the message line. I fired off an apologetic response and tried to fill her in on my life without mentioning Luka or fairgrounds or any of that. You'd think there would be nothing else to say, but it just felt good to be communicating with someone who really knew me, like taking off a pair of tight shoes and putting on slippers.

Then I sat back and thought about the real reason I was at the computer.

I typed *TMS Knitwear* into Google but nothing came up. But when I typed in *Lex McAllistair*, a flashy website popped up for McAllistair Holdings. I scrolled through until I found a picture of a large team of people all smiling and waving at the camera. At the front was Lex, with his arms folded, looking smug. The very same man who now had a big imprint of my teeth on his hand. I shivered, thinking about the car following me home.

Most of the website covered the properties he owned throughout Kent, but when I clicked on *Other business interests* I found a list of various small factories, including one TMS Knitwear.

Finally I typed the word *Bluebird* into Google. There were tons of things with that name. Loads of restaurants. An RSPB page about the actual birds. A South American tampon. Halfway down the page, though, something caught my eye.

Project Bluebird. Working to free oppressed peoples from modern slavery. I clicked on the link and the screen opened with a graphic of a bluebird trapped in barbed wire. It fluttered pathetically and then a pair of cupped hands swooped down to free it. The bird flew away to the edge of the screen and the homepage came up. I started reading.

Project Bluebird works to eliminate all forms of slavery around the world. Millions of men, women and children around the world are forced to lead lives as slaves. Although this exploitation is often not called slavery, the conditions are the same. People are sold like objects, forced to work against their will for little or no pay and are at the mercy of their 'employers', who often hold onto their passports and tell workers that they will be punished if they go to the authorities.

I thought about the passports in the safe and how the girl, Lili, seemed so scared of the bloke who worked with Lex. Was that what was going on in the marina and the knitwear factory? *Slavery?* Did Eva find out, and was that why they hounded her and Luka into the sea?

'Don't mind me, I'm just getting some clean trousers for Dylan. He's had a bit of a wee accident.'

I yelped. I hadn't even heard Will until he came into the room. I hastily closed down the screen. 'It's okay. I'm done,' I said, heart hammering.

'Are you sure? You can have as long as you like,' said Will.

'No,' I said. 'I think I've seen enough.'

It felt like pieces of a puzzle were coming together. The factory and the marina were both owned by Lex McAllistair. Hadn't they said on the news that the marina was massively over budget and late being built? Maybe this was how they were getting it done, by using slave labour just like he did in his factory. The places on that piece of paper must be the ports where the people were brought in.

I started trembling all over. I knew I should go to the police but I didn't have a scrap of real evidence. Who was going to believe a fourteen-year-old girl when you were up against someone powerful like McAllistair? I thought about telling Mum everything and then imagined how hysterical she'd be when she heard about me being followed from the marina. Plus, I couldn't really tell her about Luka.

And what would happen to me and Mum if we did

try and expose what was going on? Would they try and get rid of us the way they got rid of Eva and Luka? I pictured Luka then, cold and alone in the fairground, and had to hug myself to stop the tremors zigzagging through me. I wanted to run straight to him, to hold him and tell him what I'd found out. But how would he react if I did? Hadn't he told me quite plainly he didn't want me?

Chapter 25

Lili

First thing the next morning, Mum dragged me into town to pick up the last bits and pieces for school. As we walked through Slumpton, I seemed to have a heightened sense of the people around me. I found myself noticing them in a new way and picking up different accents or other languages. I tried to imagine what it would be like to come here when you didn't speak English and were forced to work through fear and bullying. I'd never exactly felt lucky, especially having to move to this dump with my family falling to pieces around me, but maybe I had more than I realised.

We had to queue for ages in the post office. I was staring out the window, wrestling with thoughts about seeing Luka, when a small figure scurrying by made me do a double-take.

It was that girl, Lili – the one from the factory.

I dashed outside, without even telling Mum where I was going and saw the girl heading down an alley opposite the bank.

'Lili!' I hadn't meant to shout quite so loud and the effect was like an electric shock. She turned, stumbling against the wall and stared at me with wide, dark eyes, pulling the collar of her cheap, thin coat closer around her neck.

I felt like a giant next to her, she was so small and delicate. With her dark hair and high cheekbones, she looked a bit like Eva and I wondered if she was Croatian too.

'You know my name?' she whispered, her eyes fearful. 'What you want?'

'It's OKAY,' I said. 'I just want to talk.' She was breathing heavily, blinking, like a cornered animal. 'You knew Eva, didn't you?'

The effect was instant. Her eyes filled up with tears and she nodded, wordlessly.

'How did you know her?' I said gently.

'We have cleaning job,' she said.

I remembered Luka saying his mum worked in lots of different places. Lili must have confided in Eva when they worked together.

'She try to help me but now she dead,' she said bluntly, lifting her chin defiantly. 'I dead too if I speak to you.'

'If you come to the police with me, they'll help you, Lili,' I said and she shook her head violently.

'Policeman already know. No one help. Leave me alone.'

Before I could say another word, she turned on her heel and ran down the alley.

I walked back to the post office in a daze. Lili said something about the police already knowing what was going on. Who were you supposed to go to if even the police here were rotten?

Then I thought about Mum's new boyfriend Will being a journalist. Maybe I could tell him and he could write a big story about it. But there was still no proof, especially if people like Lili were too scared to talk. It was all hopeless and I'd never felt so powerless in my life.

Mum gave me grief about dashing out and I just mumbled something about seeing someone I knew. I wasn't really listening anyway.

I was so distracted I didn't notice Abbie until she was right next to us.

'Oh hello, love!' said Mum.

'Hi, Mrs Adamson,' she said politely. 'Hi, Bel.'

I smiled and Mum grimaced. 'Please, call me Helen.'

Abbie was looking at me curiously. 'I'm just going to meet some friends from school in a café,' she said. 'Wanna come too, Bel?'

I hesitated. I would have jumped at the chance a week ago. But my head was in such a weird place, I wasn't sure I could chat like a normal person.

'Fine by me,' said Mum, turning to me. 'You've been a bit out of sorts lately, it'll do you good.'

'Okay then, thanks,' I said. 'I will.'

We said goodbye and Mum went off in the other direction. Abbie turned to look at me as we walked towards the café.

'So I'm guessing that face you've got on is connected with the cute boy in the photograph.'

I smiled, despite myself. 'Sort of, yeah. Is it that obvious?'

She nodded. 'Yup, you've got it bad, I can tell.'

'We kind of broke up,' I said. I stopped walking and so did she. Out of nowhere, tears were blurring my vision.

Abbie's expression softened and she rooted in her coat pocket for a tissue. 'It's clean,' she said, holding it towards me.

I gratefully took it and blew my nose.

'Do you want to tell me about it?' she said.

'He . . . I . . .' I stumbled over my words. I wanted to tell her. Badly. I wanted to tell her that I'd never felt this way about anyone before and that kissing Luka had been one of the very best moments in my life. Everything had been exactly right in the world and everything bad just melted away. I wanted to tell her that Luka wasn't like any other boy I'd ever known before. Not because he was a ghost. Because he was Luka.

But I couldn't speak and I tried to breathe deeply to stop myself from dissolving into a huge puddle in front of her.

'When does he go to Newcastle?' said Abbie gently.

For a minute I was confused. Then I remembered my earlier lie. 'I don't know,' I said. 'I think it's soon.'

Something seemed to snap inside my brain like an

elastic band. Why was I wasting time nursing my stupid pride when I could be with Luka again? I knew deep down that he hadn't meant it when he told me to go. He was just frightened. Who wouldn't be in his situation? Maybe he just felt humiliated. Or maybe he just wanted to protect me . . .

Abbie squeezed my arm and we both spoke at once.

'Look, Abbie, I . . .'

'Don't you think you'd better . . . ?'

We both smiled, obviously having had the exact same thought. I felt a flush of happiness that, whatever happened, I really did have another friend in Slumpton.

'Go on,' she said. 'I'll ring your mum when I get home and say you've come back to mine for a bit. Take as long as you like.'

I felt like hugging her. 'Thanks, Abbie. You're a total star.'

'No problem,' she said. I squeezed her arm and she did a wiggly finger wave thing. '*Ciao, bella,*' she called over her shoulder. 'Don't do anything I wouldn't do.' And she was gone.

When I got near to the fairground, I realised there were lorries parked outside and a couple of bulldozers. My heart started to thud. Were they bringing it down early? Was I already too late?

I raced over to a builder sitting in one of the lorries. He was smoking a cigarette and listening to Radio One.

'Excuse me!'

He took a moment to look down and see me. 'What can I do for you, darlin'?' he said with a smile.

'Has the work on the fairground started already?' I said. 'I thought it wasn't happening until after New Year.'

'Change of plan,' he said. 'I'm just waiting for them to give me the nod and then we'll get started. I'm in no hurry. I'll be sad to see the old place go.'

'Hmm, yeah, thanks.'

He said something else but I'd started to walk away, biting on my fingernail and trying to think. The entrance was in clear view of his lorry and I couldn't just stroll in there. I pretended to carry on walking past but as soon as I got to the edge of the fence I hid just behind it. I peeked back out. My hair is always the most noticeable thing about me so I pulled my hat on down low and gradually slunk back towards the entrance. No one seemed to be looking in my direction as I got there and I fumbled in my pocket for my line of tickets . . .

. . . which weren't there. I felt like screaming in frustration. I'd seen Luka vault the gates before but he had longer legs and stronger arms than me. I had to get in somehow.

I took a deep breath and started to clamber inelegantly over the top but my coat got caught on one of the metal bars. I yanked it free and thought I heard something behind me but then I was in. I could just make out a small group of men standing at the far end, walking around and writing things down. I kept to the shadows and scurried towards the ghost train.

I didn't dare work the lights so I walked into the gloom.

'Luka!' I called in a loud whisper, starting to shake with adrenaline and fear.

I heard a rustling from the back and there he was, standing in front of me looking pale and tired but just as gorgeous as I remembered.

His face lit up with a huge smile. We rushed into each other's arms. I needn't have worried about what I was going to say to him because there was no speaking at all for ages.

When we stopped kissing, he held me close and I heard him whisper, 'Bel' into my hair, as though checking I was really there.

We broke apart all too soon and then stood a bit awkwardly, despite what had just happened. Unsaid words seemed to pile up in front of us.

Luka broke the silence first. 'I'm sorry about what I said before,' he said. 'I got myself into a state over Christmas. I didn't really mean any of that stuff.'

'I know,' I said quietly. 'I should have been more understanding.'

'It's *so* good to see you,' he said. 'I thought . . . I thought you might not . . .'

And then he just grabbed me and enveloped me in his arms and we were kissing all over again.

Finally we stopped.

'You know what's happening out there, don't you?' I said and he nodded.

'Yeah, figured I'd stay in here until they pulled it down

around my head. They're starting with the rollercoaster anyway. I've been watching.' He hesitated before speaking again. 'There's something else too,' he said, with a frown. 'Take a look at this.'

He held out his hands and I jumped back about ten miles.

'What the hell is wrong with them, Luka?' I squeaked.

They were transparent. You could see the outline of his fingers, but they looked like the outside of a bubble, or oil on water. There was a sort of shimmery effect, with different colours, but when I put one finger out to touch them, they felt normal. 'I appear to be fading, from the fingers up,' he said.

'I can see that! But why?'

'I don't know.' When he finally looked at me properly, I could see the fear in his eyes. 'I think I must be dying. Except I'm already dead.'

I could do nothing but stare at him in horror.

'At first I thought maybe it had something to do with the anniversary coming up.' He was trying to speak normally but I could hear the quiver in his voice. 'Then when they started taking some of the stuff away, I realised . . .'

'. . . What?'

'I think I'm only here as long as the fairground is here, Bel,' he said quietly. 'It's all tied up somehow. I started getting weaker when they took the rides away. And then this . . .' he waggled his arms in disgust, '. . . happened.'

All I wanted to do was hold him and make it not true.

But if he was right, time was running out. I knew I had to tell him everything. And fast.

'Look, Luka,' I began, 'I think I know what it was your mum discovered.'

For the next few minutes I told him all about the marina, the passports, the factory and Lili.

He groaned when I'd finished. 'That's exactly the kind of thing Eva would get furious about. She hated any kind of injustice.' He looked at the ground for a moment, lost in his thoughts, and then cleared his throat.

'I've got some stuff to tell you too,' he said. 'Things have been coming back to me . . . about that night.'

He swallowed and I could tell the memory was hard for him.

'Go on,' I said softly, 'if you want to, that is.'

'Yeah, I do,' he said. 'I want to tell you.' He leaned back against the wall, hands in pockets, and looked at the ground. 'I'd been at my mate Dom's. I only nipped back to borrow some cash but Eva went mad when I came in, pulling me through the door and ranting at me being late. She said, "Go up to your room and pack your stuff, we're going away". I laughed and then realised she was dead serious. I started to say I wasn't going anywhere and she went nuts at me.'

He went quiet.

'What happened next?' I whispered.

'I went upstairs and stuffed a couple of dirty T-shirts off my floor into a bag. I didn't really believe we really going away.'

He took a deep breath.

'The weather had been really bad all that day and it was hammering down by the time we got into the car. We came here first, to the fairground, and I realised she had some sort of package on the back seat. She made me stay in the car while she went into the fairground and she came back without the package. She wouldn't tell me what she'd done with it. We started driving away and we realised there were headlights behind us. She put her foot down and the car behind us speeded up too. It was trying to force us off the road.'

'Was it a black 4x4?' I said and he nodded. 'With a number plate that read *MCA 2*?'

'Yeah, why?'

I told him, my heart thumping at about a million beats a minute.

'Right,' Luka continued. 'Sounds like them. So we came down to the crossroads at the bottom of the hill and then everything happened really fast. There was this massive thump and then I couldn't work out why my seat was in a funny position. Then I realised it was because the car was flying through the air. All the lights went out and we hit something else. I remember banging on the glass, really scared, and seeing the water level rise outside the window. Next thing I knew, I was watching the ambulance people hovering over Mum and people were talking about getting our car out of the sea.'

He paused and I took hold of his hand, which was trembling. He stared at the ground, as though watching the scene again in his mind's eye. When he looked up, he gave a wobbly out-breath as though trying to control himself.

'It sounds awful, Luka,' I said in a shaky voice. I couldn't bear to think what he'd been through. 'I'm so sorry.'

He squeezed my hand back, almost like he was comforting me.

'I think she must have had some sort of evidence and she hid it here in the fairground,' he said, 'but I've looked everywhere, even —'

In that moment, we heard voices outside and Luka stopped.

'Quick, come this way,' he whispered and pulled me by the hand past the cars and into the ghost train. We stumbled against the wall and in disgust I batted away something feathery that touched my face, envisaging that huge cobweb I'd seen. But Luka seemed to know exactly where to go, despite the thick darkness surrounding us.

We stopped and I realised we were where I'd heard the whispering before. I wasn't scared of that any more. I was more scared about what the living were capable of.

Luka started fumbling with his keys.

'What are you doing?' I hissed and he shushed me. I heard the key turn and the wall suddenly gave way. I realised there was a door there all along. He pulled me inside and then closed the door, fumbling for a light switch. The room was illuminated by a single dusty light-bulb that swung a little, sending slices of orange light across the gloom.

It looked like a disused storeroom. There were loads of levers and piles of metal plus some bits of other rides, including a starey-eyed lion head attached to a small seat, which looked like it came from a carousel for small kids. There were also a few bits and pieces from the ghost train, like a mouldering King Kong costume and a pile of plastic skeleton parts.

'I never knew this was here until yesterday,' said Luka quietly. 'I just discovered it. It's completely hidden unless you know about it. But I've found some fag ends and they were Mum's brand. She smoked these smelly French ones. So she obviously knew it was here too.'

I started to say something and he guessed what was coming. 'And yeah, I've looked everywhere and found nothing.'

The floor was covered in large thick boards and as I went to move forward I stumbled.

'Whoa,' I said, righting myself. I stood still for a moment and then gave a gentle jump. I could feel that the floor was sort of springy. Mind racing, I got down on my knees, trying to prise away the edge of the board.

'What are you doing?' said Luka.

'Give me a hand,' I said.

He got down beside me. With a heave, we both pulled the board at the same time and it came away in our hands. There was a small space in the earth below it. We exchanged glances and then Luka reached down with his hand to feel around. His eyes widened and he lay down on the boards flat so he could get more of his arm in there. He gasped and then it emerged, holding a thick brown A4 envelope.

'Quick, let's see what's in there!' I said and with fumbling fingers Luka opened the envelope and pulled out a handful of photos and some paper.

Several of the pictures showed foreign people with black eyes and other injuries. One man was holding up his T-shirt to reveal a deep bruise across his belly. Another showed a pile of passports in the open safe I'd seen. There was a picture of a room where people were crammed into a small space, lying in sleeping bags. The walls were peeling and damp and it looked horrible. The next picture showed Lex McAllistair arriving at a house with boarded-up windows and looking over his shoulder as he opened the door.

'I bet that's where lots of the slave workers live,' I said quietly and Luka nodded.

'Yeah, and I bet it's a house owned by that scumbag.'

One of the sheets of paper had foreign names on it and bank details with sums of money written on, most of them three or four hundred pounds. It didn't make much sense to me but the final piece of paper did. It was a letter, written in broken English.

I am being held in this contry aganst my wil. I was brot here to work and told I wold make mony for my family but since here my passport taken and I am prisner. Many more lik me at 77 and 78 Manley road. My name is Lili Babic.

I looked at Luka excitedly. 'That's her,' I said, 'the girl I told you about.'

'Right, well, guard this with your life,' said Luka, putting the stuff back into the envelope. I had no bag to put it in so I undid my coat and put the envelope inside my jumper, tightening my belt round it to keep it safe.

'What now?' I said.

'I'm going to try and get you safely out of here,' he said.

CHAPTER 26

I Don't Want to Say Goodbye

He opened the door a crack and then grabbed my hand and pulled me outside. Loud bangs and metallic screeches filled the air. I flinched at every noise, but Luka moved in a purposeful way, holding my hand tightly as he led me through the darkness and back towards the entrance of the ghost train.

When we got there, Luka gently held me back against the wall before sticking his head out. I almost cried out until I remembered that only I could see him.

'There are loads of workmen milling about now and I can't tell if McAllistair is there but there are some blokes with clipboards standing near the rollercoaster.

They've got cranes and stuff starting to break it apart. Look, Bel, I'm going to create a distraction and I want you to run for the exit gates the second I've got their attention. Got that?'

'Yeah, but what are you going to do, Luka?' I said. 'Don't do anything dangerous!' My voice went into a squeak. We both knew it was a stupid thing to say, but instead of mocking me, he just gently put his finger on my lips and then leaned over and kissed me. He looked intently into my eyes then – his own looked so dark and serious that I felt my throat tighten with fear as the selfish realisation washed over me that *he* couldn't get hurt but I could.

Just then, there was a massive clang of metal as a section of the rollercoaster's tracks was pulled away. We both jumped and even Luka looked unnerved by it.

'Look, I'm going first because I want to make sure I get their attention. You make a run for it as soon as I'm gone.' He skimmed my lips with his one more time, squeezed me hard and then ran out into the fairground. He was a fair bit away from me when he turned and said something like, 'I'll see you at the . . . !' but it was so noisy his words were swallowed up.

'Luka!' I hissed. 'I don't know where to meet you!'

But I was speaking to myself because he'd already gone. For a second I was so filled with panic at being alone that I wanted to curl into a ball on the ground and just hide.

There was no way they would hurt a teenage girl in

front of all those people, but I knew exactly what McAllistair was capable of and if he saw me here, this town could be seriously dangerous for me and Mum. He knew where I lived. I thought about Mum pottering about at home, thinking I was safely with Abbie and I almost sobbed.

I knew I had to move, even though my feet felt like lead weights. I took several deep breaths and then forced myself out of the entrance to the ghost train, a step at a time. There were plenty of people around but most of them seemed to be focusing on the rollercoaster. The noises it made as it was dismantled were like the cries of a huge dying beast and sadness washed over me that no one would ever ride on it again. The whole fairground with all its memories would soon be smashed into the dust.

I put my head down and started to scurry fast towards the exit, stepping round huge piles of plaster and metal. The turnstiles at the exit had been ripped out so there was just a gaping hole now. Relief bloomed in my chest. I was almost there, I just had to get across one last bit.

I started to move forwards again.

It was then that I saw that the same black 4x4 was parked right outside and a tall man in a long grey coat was unfolding himself from the driver's seat. Of course, it would be easier to come in that way now. I froze, just like they say rabbits do in headlights, at the exact moment he looked up.

He didn't speak or call out, which was somehow even

more scary. His expression didn't change that much at all. I turned around and started to run the other way back into the fairground and soon heard the thump of his heavy feet behind me. I was almost back to the ghost train but was so scared that I didn't notice the debris until my foot made contact and I was flying through the air in slow motion before I smashed down in the dirt.

A rough hand hauled me to my feet and I was looking into McAllistair's furious face. My knee was throbbing and felt wet but I didn't dare look at it. I couldn't look away from the cold eyes in front of me.

'What the hell do you want? Why are you always snooping around?' I could smell the smoke on his breath and even felt a fine spray of spit.

I couldn't think of a single thing to say, so I just tried to wriggle free but his grip was unbelievably strong.

'I'm going to take you to my car and we're going to have a little chat, young lady,' he said. 'I want to know what it is you think you're up to.'

A group of men in hard hats came round the corner and one of them made a questioning face to McAllistair, who shouted something about 'vandals' and just carried on pushing me towards the exit.

But then I heard someone cry out in shock and, although McAllistair didn't loosen his grip, he stopped and turned. The ground seemed to be rumbling and I looked around in confusion, not understanding what was going on until one of the men near us shouted to McAllistair.

'Some idiot's turned the 'coaster on!'

I looked up and realised that the cars on the rollercoaster had started to move along the tracks even though a huge section had been taken away. Lots of people started shouting in panic then and several of the men ran over to try and turn it all off before the cars reached the broken section. But there was no time. The cars suddenly shot forward and there was a moment where every single person just stared as the first one shot off the end, dragging the rest behind it in a long, deadly ribbon. Then everything just went mad around me. McAllistair let go of my arm and people were running in panic in all directions to get away from the cars smashing down like missiles. There was smoke and flames and confusion and I took my chance and ran as fast as I could towards the exit and out.

I kept running until I was far along the promenade and had to stop to pull in my breath, my chest aching. I could hear sirens in the distance and still see a plume of smoke rising above the fairground.

I hugged myself, shivering hard. Luka had created a distraction all right. I just hoped no one had got hurt in there, not that I cared that much if it was Lex McAllistair. I sat down on a bench and looked at the sea, still trying to get my breath back and cursing myself for not having heard what Luka had said about where he would meet me.

Where would he go? What other place *could* he go? I felt angry with him then, especially because if his theory was right, then maybe the destruction of the fairground would bring things to an end for him even sooner.

I gasped as a realisation fizzed through me.

Luka would go to the place where it all ended the first time. I just knew it.

A sick feeling of dread curdled in my stomach. I didn't want to see where he'd died. It made it all too real. But I somehow knew this was where I'd find him. I just had to go there now.

An old man was shuffling along nearby and I ran up to him, making him start. My hair was wild and I realised I probably looked a sight. I tried to smile in an unthreatening way so I didn't frighten him off.

'Sorry to bother you, but can you tell me where St Lawrence's Headland is, please?'

'Well, now . . .' He proceeded to go into an incredibly long-winded description. I wanted to shake him and was practically hopping with impatience but I soon got the gist and was able to thank him and get away. It was about a ten-minute walk and the drizzly rain started to come down much more heavily. I could feel it creeping down the back of my neck and my hair was sticking to my face like rats' tails. But I didn't care any more. I just wanted to see Luka.

Following the old man's instructions, I soon came to a bend in the road and saw where a long section of cliff jutted right out over the sea. There was a broken fence with orange netting across it and a sign said, *Danger: Cliff Erosion*. I thought about Luka and Eva's car smashing across here and falling into the sea. I turned round and looked inland. Sure enough, there was a road which could well have been the one they would have travelled down on that awful night, just as Luka had described. The thought of it made me feel sick and shaky. It was too late to make any of that right, but if I didn't see him again, I didn't think I could bear it.

I climbed over the fence, wincing at my cut knee, which was bleeding through my jeans. It was raining properly now and I shielded my face and looked out towards the sea, which was pounding furiously against the rocks, the rain slanting into it like millions of long needles.

There was a bench right on the edge of the cliff. I guessed that before the cliff eroded, it had been much further inland. I walked carefully towards it and saw it was still safe enough, just about. Trembling with exhaustion, I sat down and tried to examine my throbbing knee.

'Hey.'

I jumped up and turned to see Luka. He was just standing there and, although he smiled, there was something serious in his face that stopped me from going to him.

'Quite the stunt you pulled back there,' I said, a bit stupidly.

'I couldn't think of anything else,' said Luka. 'Are you okay? They didn't see you, did they?'

'I'm okay,' I said quietly.

We stood in silence for a second. The rain had made Luka's hair cling to his face and his eyes looked darker than ever. I realised with a jolt there was wetness in them that wasn't rain.

'Bel . . .' he said, and for a minute I wanted to cover my ears and scream that I didn't want to hear it. He stepped forward and took my hands, searching my face with his eyes. 'You know that it's nearly time, don't you?'

'You can't know that,' I wailed but he just smiled sadly.

'I do. You know why I know.' He pulled his collar away from his throat and I could see the same shimmery effect I'd seen before. It had spread. I reached out and touched where his throat met his collarbone and, although it was still solid, his skin made the tips of my fingers shiver.

'Aren't you frightened?' I said, not caring about the tears that were starting to spill down my cheeks.

'No, I'm really not. I feel tired now. Meeting you has been, well, just the best thing. But we both knew it couldn't really last, didn't we?'

Then he pulled me close and we kissed for a long time, our faces wet with rain and tears. When we broke apart, I saw that Luka was looking over my shoulder at something. His eyes went wide and then he gave a sad smile.

'What is it, Luka?' I turned and with a jolt realised that in the mist along the cliff was a small dark-haired woman, standing with her feet neatly together.

I gasped. 'Is that her?' I whispered and Luka nodded.

He leaned down and kissed me again and I clung onto him.

'I don't want you to go yet!' I cried out but he gently pulled away from me.

'I have to, Bel. I have to go. You know that.'

'Okay, but don't say goodbye. I can't stand to hear you say goodbye.' I was babbling nonsense now but it seemed that if I didn't hear the word, maybe it wouldn't be quite so true. 'You'd better just go.'

He pulled me into his arms one last time and squeezed me so hard I couldn't breathe. I heard him whisper, 'Bel,' again, then he let go of me and started to walk away. I bowed my head and rain dripped off my chin but I couldn't stop myself from looking.

Eva and Luka both started to run at the same time. I heard her cry out, 'Luka, baby!' and he enveloped her in his arms.

The rain was coming so heavily now that it was hard to see. I went to wipe my eyes with my sleeve and closed them for a split second, but when I opened them again there was no one there at all standing on the cliff.

I was completely alone.

CHAPTER 27

Gone

I ran over to where they'd been standing and shouted, 'Luka!' into the wind.

I knew it was pointless. He was gone. But my brain couldn't accept it.

I murmured, 'No, no, no, no,' over and over again, gulping hot tears and then I found myself sinking down onto my knees, my arms wrapped round myself as sobs shuddered through me.

Squeezing my eyes tightly shut, I thought about the moment when we'd kissed for the first time, already a lifetime ago, and the way he'd laced his fingers through mine right before our lips met. I tried to picture it all, to hang onto that moment, but all I could see was the image of him running towards Eva and out of my life.

I couldn't believe I'd never see him again, or touch him . . . it was so unfair and wrong I didn't think I could stand it. I always thought heartache was just a figure of speech but I really had a pain in my chest and it hurt, it hurt so much.

I lost all track of time but after what could have been minutes or an hour, I noticed something lying in the grass next to me. It was Luka's keys. I fumbled for them with my numb fingers and pressed them to my lips. Having something of his helped calm me a little and after a few moments I got to my feet and groped for a tissue to wipe my wreck of a face. As my hand went into my pocket, a horrible realisation went through me like an electric shock . . .

. . . *Guard this with your life* . . .

I couldn't feel the package. I gave out a moan as I frantically felt inside my top. But it was gone.

I ran to the main road and headed back in the direction I'd come from. I didn't dare go all the way to the fairground as I could hear the fire engines there, but I went as far as I could, scanning the ground desperately.

Eventually I slowed to a stop, almost blinded by tears, my shoulders heaving. It was no good.

Stupid, stupid, stupid . . .

After all we'd gone through to find it, it was lost.

Luka and Eva had died for nothing.

I was wet through and almost delirious with sadness and cold. I don't even remember how I got home. But when I did, Mum was furious with me for being in such a state and kept questioning me over and over about what I'd been doing. I insisted I'd left Abbie's and gone for a walk on the beach. I made up some rubbish about tripping over a rock.

Mum clearly didn't believe that for a second, but there wasn't a lot she could do about it. Eventually she realised I had a raging temperature and sent me off to bed where I cried quietly for ages until I eventually passed out.

I didn't do much else but sleep for twenty-four hours straight.

When I finally woke up properly, I thought for a minute I'd died. The room was bathed in a white glow and everything was muffled and quiet. I had the mad thought that I was in heaven and Luka would be there too. Then I saw the uneaten toast and cup of cold tea on my bedside table. I got out of bed cautiously and drew back the curtain.

The world had been transformed while I was asleep. Every surface was thickly covered in snow that sparkled in the winter sunshine. It looked just like a Christmas card. Normally I would have been excited, but I hurt all over, like someone had peeled back my skin and all my nerve endings were on red alert.

I sat back on the bed. All I could think about was Luka, going over the last time I saw him, again and again. Could he really be gone, just like that? When I thought about losing the package, a sick shame twisted inside me.

I wanted to see his face badly then and started tossing

all my clothes around, desperately trying to look for the jeans I'd been wearing that day. I knew I'd put the picture in my pocket that morning. I cursed Mum because I realised she'd have taken everything for the wash. Then I noticed she'd made a neat little pile of stuff from my pockets on my chest of drawers. The keys and keyring were there under some crumpled paper and the picture of Luka, right on the top in an obvious way.

I knew there would be questions about these items. She was obviously just waiting until I was better until she could interrogate me.

I curled back into bed, threading the keyring into one fist as I examined Luka's face, wishing I could fix it in my mind. I kissed the photo and then held it against my heart, my eyes tightly closed. He was already fading. I knew that it wouldn't be long until he was just a vague image, however much I tried to cling onto his memory.

I swallowed hard and absently twisted the keyring in my fingers. Luka said it was a Croatian good luck charm. It hadn't brought him and Eva much luck, that was certain. Looking at it properly for the first time, I realised the head of the little doll unscrewed. I expected to find a smaller doll inside but when I pulled the two pieces apart I realised something else was there instead.

Something that looked like the memory card from a camera.

A smile broke across my face.

CHAPTER 28

Here Is the News

South Kent News
Page last updated at 04:50 GMT,
Slavery Ring Found in Sleepy Kent Resort
Kent police have uncovered a 'significant' people-trafficking ring in the rundown seaside resort town of Slumpton. Raiding a series of businesses and construction projects, including a multimillion pound marina development, they found up to 120 migrant workers living in squalid conditions from a variety of countries including Croatia, China and Pakistan.

Passports had been confiscated on arrival to the UK and most victims were told they had to repay large sums of money to the parties who brought them here.

A local millionaire and businessman, Alexander

McAllistair, and a number of senior councillors have been arrested and are being held for questioning under the Anti-People Trafficking Act 2007.

The story first appeared in local newspaper The Slumpton Advertiser. *Senior Reporter Will Longmeadow told us, 'I can't reveal my sources but I received incriminating images implicating powerful local figures. I immediately went to the highest authorities.'*

A spokesperson from the anti-slavery charity Project Bluebird said, 'There is no place for slavery in the modern world and we hope to see the men behind this brought to justice.'

I didn't get to look at what was on the memory card. I took a chance that something important had to be on there, for Eva to hide it like she did. And I was right. She had photographed everything, including Lili's letter. Will never actually knew who his source was because I sent it all anonymously, with carefully altered handwriting. There was no other way. I shuddered at the very thought of explaining it all to Mum. And how would anyone ever understand about Luka?

What Will found on the memory card was like a stick of dynamite in the middle of Slumpton. Not long after the story was on the news, McAllistair was on bail, waiting for his criminal trial. A local policeman and a couple of town councillors were also found to be part of the smuggling ring.

I never found out what happened to Lili. I liked to imagine that she was back with her family again and no longer so scared and timid. But maybe she would never get over it.

The worst bit was knowing that the truth about what happened to Luka and Eva would probably never come out. There was just nothing to prove their part of the story. It seemed desperately unfair that McAllistair and his men wouldn't be charged with murder. Because that's what it had been. But at least we'd stopped them ruining anyone else's life.

There was a silver lining though. I saw something in the local paper about how some photographs of the fairground had been found and it seems they've gone to the local museum. They're going to be used as part of an exhibition about the town's history.

So Eva got her exhibition after all.

Luka would have been so proud.

Luka . . .

Every time I thought about him walking away into the rain, I went through that goodbye all over again.

I would have done anything to be allowed to see him one last time.

CHAPTER 29

Spring

Five months later

'Bel! You'd better get a move on, or you'll be late on the first day back!'

'I'm *coming!*'

I finish off tying the David Stafford tie. (Still purple. Still horrible.)

I look at my reflection in the mirror and make a face, before heading off down the stairs.

I see Mum at the hall mirror, her mouth stretched into a square as she applies her lipstick. She often wears lipstick these days, and she's just had her hair cut and coloured. She doesn't have that pinched look any more either.

'Now, you know I'm going out tonight, don't you?' she says.

'How could I forget?' I reply. 'You've been going on about it all week.'

'Oi, missy, watch it,' she says and tries to smack me on the bum as I duck into the kitchen.

A bowl of cereal later, I'm out the door, off for the first day of the second half of the summer term.

The sun isn't exactly cracking the pavement and I still can't imagine anyone ever actually sitting on the beach, but the trees are all bunchy with blossom and the air smells nice. Slumpton seems only averagely rubbish these days, rather than the worst place in the world.

There have been quite a few changes since everything that happened at Christmas.

Dad lives in Newcastle now. And that's all right. It took me a while, don't get me wrong. Eventually I agreed to visit but said I didn't want anything to do with his other woman and he respected that and kept her out of the way. By the third visit, I decided it was time to put him out of his misery. Can't say I adore her. But she's all right. I'll live.

Mum's seeing Will properly. He has turned out to be okay. He got promoted after breaking that story. Sometimes I feel like asking for a commission.

There's even talk about bringing back the fairground now the marina project has been scaled down.

I don't think I'll be going though. Too many memories there for me.

I think about Luka all the time. I still miss him so much and sometimes I get the shivers so hard I have to sit down. I wonder, 'Why me?' Why was I the only person who could see him? I guess I'll never really know.

I've even wondered whether I really *did* meet a ghost boy at all or if I had some kind of nervous breakdown, brought on by the stress of moving here and my parents splitting up.

But I know that's not true. And I only have to look at the photo to remember how it felt to be in his arms, to kiss him, to see his face light up as he smiled at me.

If I think about it all too much I get a bit dizzy and worry I'll turn into some sort of nutter. It's time to concentrate on the living.

Abbie's waiting at the end of the street so we can walk to school together and I give her a wave. She casually waves back. She's not one to get excited about anything much. Her laid-back attitude makes me laugh and makes me a little bit envious too. She probably wouldn't blink if I told her the truth about what happened at Christmas.

But I know I never will.

As I'm walking towards her, an ice-cream van goes by and all the hairs on my arms stand up. It's playing the tune I heard on the carousel the day I met Luka.

I stare after it for a moment and wonder . . .

Stop it, Bel, I think. *He's gone.* I swallow deeply and, for a second, a pain in my chest makes me gasp.

'Hey,' says Abbie, with a grin.

'Hey,' I say back, giving myself a shake.

'Ready for the shiny new term?' She raises an eyebrow in that clever way she has.

'Yeah,' I say. 'Bring it on.'

Acknowledgements

I'd like to thank the following people:

Helenanne Hansen and Michele Kirsch for being early readers of *Dark Ride* and giving me the encouragement and courage to stick with it.

Suzy Greaves for her stubborn belief this would happen for me one day.

Luisa Plaja, Emily Gale, Alexandra Fouracres and Sam Tonge for mopping me up a million times and providing the best writerly support a girl could ask for.

My dad, George Green, for giving me the writing gene in the first place.

Paul Donohoe from the real 'Project Bluebird.' Antislavery is a charity that fights against people trafficking and slavery worldwide. Donations can be made via their website www.antislavery.org.

Everyone at Piccadilly Press but especially Anne Clark for rescuing me from the slush pile and being the kind of editor I always dreamed of working with one day.

Finally and most importantly of all, thanks and love to Pete, Joe and Harry for being there through thick and thin.

piccadillypress.co.uk

Go online to discover

☆ more exciting books you'll love

☆ competitions

☆ sneak peeks inside books

☆ fun activities and downloads

☆ and much more!